The John Simmons Short Fiction Award

Line of Fall

MILES WILSON

UNIVERSITY OF IOWA PRESS

IOWA CITY

University of Iowa Press, Iowa City 52242
Printed in the United States of America
First edition, 1989

Some of these stories have previously appeared, in a slightly altered form, in the
*Iowa Review, Georgia Review, Southwest Review, Writers' Forum, Texas Review, Kansas
Quarterly, Indiana Review, New Mexico Humanities Review, Passages North,* and *New
Growth: Contemporary Short Stories by Texas Writers.*

The publication of this book is supported by a grant from the National Endowment
for the Arts in Washington, D.C., a federal agency.

Library of Congress Cataloging-in-Publication Data

Wilson, Miles.
Line of fall/Miles Wilson.—1st ed.
p.   cm.—(The John Simmons short fiction award)
ISBN 0-87745-259-8 (alk. paper)
I. Title.   II. Series.
PS3573.I4598L5   1989   89-36788
813'.54—dc20   CIP

For Brittany, Clare, and Vicki

and for Bren and Anna

Contents

Wyoming

McGrath had been driving three days, I-80 all the way from Indiana into the breadbasket of an ugly blizzard that gave him something to think about. One day to Council Bluffs, one more to Cheyenne, and now sluicing in the wake of a Redball Express rig somewhere west of Laramie. He had caught the truck on a sweeping climb east of Elk Mountain and decided to tuck in behind. Now, even with chains, he wouldn't be able to get around; the north lane had drifted in to wall him off.

McGrath checked the gauges. It seemed prudent, but he knew that probing invited bad luck, his attention wiring the Volvo into the socket of his uneasiness. Skip, a philosopher-mechanic in Bloomington who worked only on Peugeots and Saabs, had debugged the electrical system as a favor to a friend. More precisely, Skip had promised only to induce the bugs to migrate into redundant circuitry where, left undisturbed, they might remain. Skip was of the opinion that Volvo built a good marine diesel and that their electrical systems had been designed by a German engineer who subscribed to Gurdjieffian electrokinetics and had never forgiven the Swedes their neutrality in World War II. Skip had spent three days drinking akvavit and reading Schopenhauer in preparation for the job.

The Volvo belonged to McGrath's wife, who now belonged to someone else. They had bought it from a colleague in the English Department at Bowling Green to which McGrath also no longer belonged. He was driving to San Francisco, to the MLA Convention, for an interview with Jenijoy LaBelle—Vonnegut, Fielding, Margaret Mitchell?—about a one-year replacement position at Long Beach State.

The Redball's logo was right in his face, and McGrath dropped into second as they squared off with another hill. McGrath had figured wrong. A Brown Ph.D., six years of carving up his dissertation into articles, servicing the department, tight with a couple of senior professors and cordially suppressing his gag reflex with most of the rest. Even that last year when suddenly, inexplicably, it all hung in the balance, sending

3

off to that outfit in Boston that filled in, at five dollars a whack, blank student evaluations in a variety of inks and handwriting and with whatever comments you sent along. And it had come to this: adrift in academe, out of it now for a semester, willing to take even a migrant labor job, stooping over rows of freshman essays: "In our modern world of today everyone has their own opinions about life." Jenijoy LaBelle—Poe, Tom Robbins, Ringling Brothers?

A cornice of ice broke off the back of the truck and McGrath swerved sluggishly, missing the chunk with his tire but taking a thick whump somewhere around the oil pan. The oil light remained blank and oracular. Had it worked when he started the car after gassing up in Laramie? McGrath took a slow drink of rum to shore up where the blow had caved part of his stomach in.

By one o'clock in the afternoon McGrath had made Rawlins, driving with his knuckles the last twenty miles, dervished by a ground blizzard. Snow-dazed and ringing from the slap of chains, he followed the Redball into a truck stop. Inside, he spread out the map. A hundred miles in three hours. He'd given himself two days' slack, and that was gone. He'd have to put in, say, thirty-six hours in the next forty-eight to make the interview. Already, the ache of the road had gotten beneath the husk McGrath folded into whenever he needed to make good time over long distances.

The waitress set down a cup of coffee without asking, and McGrath ordered a hamburger. He poured cream into the cup and loaded it with sugar. When the burger arrived, he layered it top and bottom with catsup and covered his mound of fries with the rest of the bottle.

Road-stunned, McGrath's eyes wandered the map. West of Rawlins, a state highway went north and stopped. No town, just stopped. A cartographer's error, bad planning, a metaphor? In Wyoming? McGrath combed his memory. No writer he knew of had ever come from the state. Pound? No, that was Idaho, or maybe Washington. Wyoming, a wind-sucked vacuum in the literary map of America. What if he took that road?

He saw the dress before he really saw the girl. An electric floral print: orchids, hibiscus—McGrath's grandmother had raised them—and half a dozen other improbable tropical exotics he couldn't name. The girl's hair was long and straight and almost the color of parchments he had seen once in the British Museum. The rest was ordinary: plain face, serviceable figure, maybe twenty-five, a springiness in her walk as she approached the register, her center of gravity not yet migrated to her hips. She paid her bill and passed across the room near his table. She saw him watching her, but he was too weary to look away. Her eyes were ash-gray and yes, she flickered a smile and went on through the doors into the alcove that buffered the room from the weather.

McGrath finished his sodden fries and left a rueful tip. In the lee of the building, the Volvo's windshield had filled with snow. McGrath unlocked the car and ducked in. In the stunted light, the girl bloomed in the passenger seat.

McGrath woke up entirely. The girl was attentive but perfectly at ease. Before McGrath could imagine what to say, while card after card skittered face down from the deck—what kind of sucker was he being played for; was this unguessed good luck; hadn't he locked the passenger side and what about his manuscript, his Leica, his Slazenger (who would play in Wyoming, how could anyone fence it?), in fact, the whole affectionate debris of his adult life piled on the seat behind him?—before he could arrange any of this into a hand he could play, the girl raised a cautionary finger and leaned forward to blow on the windshield. In a sure and elegant hand, she wrote across the pearly film:

mute
Abby
from: Abora Wells
to: west

And on the evidence of the colons and the lowercase *w*, and because he could not think of what else to do, when the girl turned from her writing and smiled again and nodded at the ignition, McGrath turned the Volvo over and they set out.

The first ten miles or so he had to settle into the weather again and the little detonations of adrenaline as the Volvo yawed, even with chains and tethered in ruts, in a wind that had shifted and now surged broadside against the car. When he had fallen into the erratic rhythm of it, he reached under his seat and took another pull from the rum. He offered the bottle and the girl tipped it up, deftly blocking the top with her fingertips. She touched her tongue to them and made an exaggerated face.

McGrath laughed. "Old Paint Stripper, specialty of the house."

The girl breathed, spun the words out of her index finger.
Find another house

The blizzard seemed to have let up some, but the wind came like a blind, enormous drunk, and the running snow had begun to drift into the open lane. It was colder now too; the Volvo's heater couldn't keep up with it. McGrath turned on the radio. KBOY gave him the price of feeder hogs in Chicago, how many head of cattle had been shipped to Omaha last week. He walked the dial across the band, then switched to FM. Poised among the static was a strong station, playing an arrangement for flute, drums, and some stringed instrument he couldn't identify. It sounded like the score for a Kurosawa film. When it was over, the DJ, his voice like a stoned dream of speaking (McGrath could be convinced that all FM stations in the country were plugged in to one announcer, operating from a Vaseline-coated sauna in Boulder, Colorado), produced the call letters KHAN, and the radio went dead. McGrath spun the dial, hoping for static. The generator light hadn't come on, and he was about to pop the cover over the fuses when the girl pointed. McGrath had to lean above the wheel to follow her finger past the crescent of compacted snow that surrounded the wipers. The antenna had snapped off, leaving an ice-crusted stub.

McGrath shrugged and worked on the bottle again. They were not making good time; at thirty-four, McGrath was not making good time.

How did you get here?

McGrath turned to look at her. He had been wrong about her eyes. They were more green than gray, the iris flecked with amber. It must have been the fluorescent lights in the truck stop.

"I-80 mostly from Bloomington. Bloomington, Indiana. I was staying with friends."

No. How did you get here?

McGrath guessed. "I used to teach. I used to be married. She took off with a graduate student, some goofy leftover from the sixties. I'm going to see about another job in California."

The same thing?

"More or less."

The girl frowned at this and settled back. McGrath's thoughts idled ahead. He wondered if they would be sleeping together that night. He tried to erect the possibilities, but his imagination was chaste as a ghost. They topped a rise and McGrath looked north. Rail lines ran along the freeway. An empty gondola car lay tilted against a bank on what must have been a siding. The snow had drifted over the lower lip of the car and was filling the cargo space. Before today, McGrath could not have believed in such a wind. The Volvo seemed suddenly like a model of itself, set down by accident in a world where the scale was terribly wrong. Where only the distance of Wyoming was proportionate to the wind and the veteran cold. The thought of it made McGrath's teeth ache.

The girl was at the windshield again, but not writing. Breathing and working, first with her finger, then her nails, and finishing the foreground with her hair spread between her fingers like a brush, she unscrolled a panorama of plains and beyond them a forest folding back into domed mountains, all of it bisected by a great river that flowed improbably from the plains away through a rift in the mountain line. McGrath scanned the detail, then took the scene in whole again. It was stylized, a pure act of imagination, yet it seemed absolutely right, more credible than a *National Geographic* diorama. It felt a little like he thought Kenya might. McGrath realized he had been holding his breath.

"Are you an artist?"

The girl leaned close to the windshield, puffed her cheeks, and blew over a spot at the river's edge. She drew a stick figure, then added an outsized head, a caricature of McGrath. The head was set on backwards, and an amplified toe of the stick man was dipped gingerly in the water. The girl put her whole face into a smile that had no referent in his inventory of expressions.

He watched the scene as little rivulets of condensation began to run and the cold ate it all away. The whole thing remained clear to him long after it was gone.

They gassed up in Wamsutter and McGrath asked the girl if she was hungry. She shook her head and they went on, into the deep afternoon, scuds of thinner gray breaking through now and then above the ground blizzard. Later, the light failing steadily, McGrath caught sight of something off to his left and no telling how many hundreds of feet up. Broadside to him, it was flat and rectangular, metallic, about the size of a house trailer. Tumbling, it disappeared until the wide surface came round again. It veered extravagantly and, before McGrath could point the girl to it, was lost in the driving snow.

The light had been gone for some time when the girl began to play. The instrument sounded like a harmonica, but with greater range and resonance. Call it a mouth organ, thought McGrath. She built the piece layer by layer, and McGrath sifted the memory of his wife's scuffed collection of classical music. Nothing stuck. When the girl was finished, he asked her.

Me

"No, I mean the composer."

Me again

"What do you call it?"

Anything you like

"But you must have a name for it, something to call it when you want to remember."

I just made it up. You give it a name for me to remember

"Wyoming."

The girl tooted her instrument like a circus calliope.

Sometime around midnight they broke over a summit after an imperceptible climb. Ahead, a rinse of lights made McGrath squint. He couldn't remember the last light he had seen. The snow was banked so that even whatever eastbound traffic there might have been was shielded from view. Closer, a gargantuan American flag stood out straight in the floodlit wind; closer still, a sign above the drifts: "Little America." McGrath played a flashlight across the map. Such a thing did exist, confirmed by Texaco.

He pulled in to gas up again. The place looked like an outpost on the moon, snow-chromed and antiseptic as an operating room. The boy who took his money told him to shuck his chains. The road west was spotty with bare pavement; he'd chew up his tires in no time. As McGrath unraveled the chains, he wondered how the place got any help. A two-story, multi-wing motel that must have had hundreds of rooms, a coffee shop the size of a school cafeteria, rank upon rank of pumps. There wasn't a town, nothing for at least fifty miles. Did Wyoming have gulags? McGrath seemed to remember that it had been a Republican state for a long time. And James Watt. Maybe Little America was staffed with bureaucrats who had fallen from his grace and been posted here—the extremity of the interior.

McGrath had to take off his gloves to manipulate the chains. When he got back in, he could barely curve his fingers around the wheel. The girl took his hands in her own, guided them under her dress. She didn't flinch when she took her hands away and closed her thighs on McGrath's glacial fingers; she didn't stiffen when he began to move them as the feeling came back. There had been something so attentive in her doing this that it drained the act of all erotic content. Bowed toward her, both palms facing away from him like a mendicant, McGrath thought he was going to weep.

When his fingers tingled, he withdrew them and felt around under the seat for the rum. And because he couldn't trust what else he might have said, he left it at "thanks."

Unchained, the Volvo skittered less than McGrath had expected. The wind settled in at a steady 20 mph or so, and the blowing snow sheeted across the road. The moon had broken out behind them, and McGrath could see patches of pavement, like a dark arctic sea, that appeared wherever the plows had gouged through the snowpack. McGrath relaxed a little. Unclenched, he felt the weariness in his thighs and back, tasted the peculiar tarnish, the transcontinental casing in his mouth. On wobbly legs, his prospects teetered west: Jenijoy LaBelle—Barth, Pynchon, Borges?

You could throw it away—let it all go

McGrath muffled the flashlight against the seat but did not turn it off.

"What?" He was afraid that he knew.

You must decide. Now, I think

"Yeah, well, I don't know." McGrath tried to pick his way. "Sure, I suppose. Why the hell not." What was a promise to her?

The cold clamped him like an imperative from the end of the earth. The girl had rolled her window down. She leaned around the bucket seat and brought up his overnight bag, setting it on the hump behind the gearshift.

Jesus, that's what she meant. She was calling him on it. McGrath swerved wildly, then leveled at once into a lunar calm.

"Why," he said steadily, "the hell not."

The girl did not respond, and McGrath drained the last of the rum.

"Well, go ahead."

You must do it

"I can't throw and steer; you drive?"

Yes

McGrath didn't need the flashlight anymore. The moon had broken through altogether and he could read by its light. He stopped the car and they squirmed around each other. McGrath looked back, checking for traffic. Only Wyoming, thirty-four years of it. And the moon, hanging like a wild ace for those whose luck had run out.

The girl went through the gears a little mechanically but without hesitation. He was, McGrath saw, in capable hands.

The whole thing went quickly. He had no urge to linger, did not look back, even as his manuscript flapped away behind them, giddy at the thought of some cowpoke turning up a weather-beaten page: "As J. Hillis Miller suggests, the self-referential nature of all structures—indeed, their deconstructive plasticity—has called into question the *logos* of 'beginning, continuity and end, of causality, of dialectical process, of organic unity, and of ground.'" The air was at him like a bibliography of pain, burning his nostrils, blurring his sight, the ache coming back to his fingers. And it was all so light in his hands as he lifted it up and turned it loose in the slipstream. He was rolling up the window when he felt her hand on him.

Everything

McGrath checked the back. "That's it."

Not quite

It came to him that he was all that was left.

The girl twisted in the seat and in a quick sweep had her dress off over her head. Under it, there was nothing else. She handed the dress to McGrath and he caught the scent of cinnamon as he let the wind take it away. Turning, he watched it blossom above the snow.

He came out of his own clothes reflectively, handling each

piece as though he had been a manikin dressed for a costume ball.

Done, McGrath leaned back in the seat and let his weariness have him. He warmed up quickly, and soon even the little spasms in his legs went away. Beside him, the girl's torso was lit like a crescent, curving into her thighs and away in the dark.

"What do you do?"

The girl arched forward.

This

McGrath rode the answer to sleep.

He woke once. The moon had shifted and was pouring over her shoulder into her lap. Sleep-sluiced, McGrath registered the amber thicket that arose there, spreading down her thighs as far as the moon lit them. He went back to sleep.

He woke again at dawn, the perimeter of light widening at his back. When she saw that he was awake, the girl eased the Volvo to the side of the road and stopped. She was wearing woolly stockings and a sheepskin coat that she must have hidden under the seat. She smiled at McGrath and was gone. He scrambled into the driver's seat and was half out the door calling "Abby, Abby," when she turned from the median and stopped him with an imperial motion of absolute command. She turned again, at the top of the driftline, made another gesture of, what—permission, benediction, regret?—and disappeared down into the eastbound lanes.

Pure forsakenness sucked at McGrath, and when it was done he feels like uncirculated silver, untarnished by handling. As he drives away, accelerating west—the Volvo skating, freelancing it over the patches of snowpack—the instrument panel lights up like a slot machine and McGrath cups his hands for the payoff. The lights go out and then McGrath is across the border—welcomed to Utah by the governor himself—and he fogs the windshield to write his name across it, his vapors retrieving part of the scene of mountain and plain, and with more of his breath brings the whole thing back with the stick man, yes, now out in the current astride a raft. And singing "Jenijoy LaBelle," McGrath cups his hands again for riches, claps for the luck of Salt Lake City as he passes through, naked and shining, a vision out of the east, and then the lake itself, the salt flats, the high desert and the Sierras and on down, all the way to the edge of America.

Everything

By the time Roger gathered that others thought something was amiss, Amanda had left, and his acquisitions, having long since filled the basement, garage, and bedrooms, were beginning to edge down the hallway towards the living room. Roger had to concede that this was arguably eccentric. Still, he felt perfectly ordinary and was frankly annoyed that anyone should think otherwise. In fact, it was Amanda, stable as the mortgage, who had been the enthusiast in the early going, prodding him from behind the sports page to track one down over by Volunteer Park that was sure to be a gold mine. Or rolling him out at 6:30 on Saturday for a crosstown run to just miss a Wedgwood service for five. What could be more wholesome than rising at dawn on the weekend to save money by spending it?

This had gone on haphazardly for some months. Gradually, Roger came to look forward to the weekends and began taking a more active role in planning their sorties. He bought a large city map and laid out their route the night before. Amanda navigated. This was agreeable at first, since Roger was level-tempered about circling back for missed cross streets. He toned up his driving techniques by quizzing pizza deliverers and taxi drivers, whose tips turned him into an assertive city motorist. And he discovered a few shortcuts on his own. At house sales, he would wheel the Subaru into the driveway, short-circuiting the fussiness of finding a parking place on the street. Besides saving time, such an arrival gave him momentum and presence. People seemed more willing to bargain. He also began to pick up the Saturday *Post-Intelligencer* at the loading dock just after midnight to get the jump on any listings that had not appeared in Friday's classifieds.

As Amanda lost interest, her navigation became more erratic, prompting several sharp quarrels and Roger's suspicion that on occasion she deliberately misled him. It was therefore agreed that Roger would solo. This did not prove immediately satisfactory, but it encouraged Roger to undertake a memory project for which his earlier work in the field—batting aver-

1 7

ages and irregular French verbs—had hardly prepared him. Over a period of months, working in twelve block grids, he developed an exact recall of all listed city streets. It occurred to him that he could win bar bets with such knowledge, but he hadn't been in a bar since he'd married.

Roger soon acquired a feel for the trade that set him apart from the dabblers. For example, he discovered that midweek sales could surprise you. Most folks couldn't get out during the week, so if you beat the pros from the secondhand stores, there were some nice deals to be made. The trick, of course, was getting out yourself. Roger worked as a technical writer for a company that prided itself on forward-looking policies such as flexible work schedules. Roger could fit in enough evening hours to mostly keep up with his work. This still didn't free up all the time he needed, but at night he was able to tap into the company mainframe to run simulated routes, cull out repeat sellers, and establish a rating system to assess the potential of any address in the city.

As Amanda grew restive, he found himself hedging about how much he'd bought. And what. Whenever he could, Roger kept his acquisitions in the trunk of the car until Amanda had gone to bed, then took them directly from garage to basement. Amanda was by turns baffled, accusatory, and finally silent about his pursuit. When it became clear that Amanda was going to let the affair run its course, Roger felt free to expand the range of his purchases, unencumbered by arguments about utility. An electric letter opener, a collection of gilded and tattooed grasshoppers, a gallon pail of assorted hex head bolts, the complete works of Schuyler Colfax, a magnum of cod-liver oil, two propane-fired coffee makers, a wizard's cape from Guinea-Bissau, and lacrosse goalie pads accumulated in snug rows across the basement.

It was a moonlight patio sale that finally propelled Amanda out of his life. Amanda's college roommate and her husband were in Seattle for a convention. They came by for dinner and an evening of catching up. After the meal and what he thought was a decent interval, Roger excused himself to pop out for a small matter that required his attention. He had trouble finding the address. The articles were disappointing, but he got a tip from one of the regulars on the tour about a midnight sale on the far south side at a disbanding theater collective. Roger felt he could trust the information and the ***½ rating; the man owed him a favor for steering him to a collection of arrangements for marimba and harpsichord.

By the time Roger returned home, Amanda's friends were gone. The lights in the house blazed fiercely, and Roger guessed there was music to be faced. He thought to postpone matters until morning, but after several lingering trips to the basement, he found Amanda still up, red-eyed but cried out, as nearly as he could judge, seated on the living room sofa.

"I can't take it anymore." Amanda's hair, never her best feature, hung about her head like a funeral wreath.

"Why couldn't you drink or gamble? Or hop in bed with Mimi Merriman? I could handle that. But this is sick. It's not normal. It's humiliating. I broke down and showed Gina and Hank. They said the right things, but I could tell. They thought I was some kind of freak for putting up with it. Like I was in on it. Oh why the hell couldn't you molest kids or something? Even *Parade Magazine* has stuff about child molesters. Nobody talks about what you're doing; there isn't even a name for it."

This all seemed somewhat out of proportion to Roger, but he reminded himself that they hadn't talked much lately and he might have misgauged the depth of her feelings in the matter. He also remembered some recent long-distance calls to her brother, who had taken an early and unprovoked dislike to Roger. Likely, Kendall's hand was visible here.

"So I'm through, done, kaput. Unless this stops, Roger, and I mean right now, I'm leaving you."

Roger puzzled over what to say, but some response was clearly required.

"I can see how you might feel that way."

That was not going to do it; the air still crackled with ozone. "I mean, maybe you could, you know, take up some little hobby of your own. I wouldn't mind."

"Some little hobby!" Amanda surged off the couch. Roger was sitting in his chair, nearly the length of the room away. Overmatched by the distance and distracted by a little stumble, Amanda stopped in the center of the room.

"Look at it this way," she said in a nasty tone that did not wear well on her. "You'll have more room when I'm gone."

Roger had to admit that she was right.

The divorce was straightforward: Amanda got the bank account, the bonds, the Buick, and his pension. Roger kept the Subaru and the house.

It seemed an appropriate time to take stock of his circumstances in case something really was out of alignment. Admittedly, his cumulative behavior was out of the ordinary, but if he was troubled at all it was because he couldn't account for his conduct. Having long thought of himself as a sort of dishwater liberal, Roger briefly entertained the notion that his interests were political. Such an appraisal displayed him to advantage: he was simply helping to mend the tattered safety net beneath the flying trapeze of runaway capitalism. On examination, however, it turned out that he rarely bought from the truly poor and bargained aggressively with them when he did. Some months before they separated, Amanda had insisted that he read a piece on compensatory behavior in *Psychology Today*. The article maintained that the repetitive sexual acquisitions of many adults were the result of emotional deprivation in their early years. The point hardly seemed to apply, as far as Roger could see. His own childhood had been serene, and while his family was not wealthy he could not recall absence or shortage.

Another possibility, of course, was some real craziness on his part. He considered those men who built houses in the

Arizona desert out of nothing but hubcaps or beer bottles. Or the eccentrics who tunneled for years beneath their property. Not that Roger saw anything essentially wrong with such behavior, but it did take one somewhat out of the mainstream. Roger, a long-standing fan of the mainstream, would not willingly leave it. That he felt as pedestrian as ever was a solid comfort. He decided he was merely doing what he wanted to do, not something he had to do. And when he wanted to do something else, he would. This seemed to him sensible and ordinary, and settled the matter as far as he was concerned. He could always rethink it if there were further developments.

On the whole, Roger felt much cozier with Amanda gone. From time to time, though, a little rinse of loneliness would dampen his spirits. At work, the technical writers were quarantined in warrens away from the roisterous engineers who were forever sabotaging each other's desks or epoxying saltshakers to the tables in the cafeteria. Their glee in such undertakings reminded Roger of his days in a college dorm. The company liked to encourage this spirited camaraderie, but had learned from Japanese consultants that writers were too sensitive or dyspeptic to participate in such corporate roughhouse. Besides, Roger worked largely at night now.

He began to feel more warmly towards the regulars on the tour. They were competitors, of course, but Roger came to see them as colleagues too, all embarked on the same great adventure. Among them was Sister Mentholatum, for whom he felt special fondness.

Her name derived from that particular ointment which she surely lathered in before donning her habit. The effect on bystanders was tonic; the spirit revived in that medicinal air. Had Sister M been a spring or cave, she long since would have been a celebrated shrine. Sister Mentholatum was detached from the Little Sisters of Topeka to minister in the spiritual wilderness of garage sales. She soon discovered a gift for acquisitions, however, and, without exploiting her position except out of Christian necessity, she began to assemble a warehouse of earthly goods. Once, in a euphoric moment, having just out-maneuvered Easy Ed himself of Easy Ed's Pawn and Tackle Shop for an upright freezer, she confided to Roger that she'd been called in a vision to prepare for the day when St. Vincent de Paul would be overthrown, having been corrupted by Vatican bankers who, having fallen on hard times, now insisted that all Church subsidiaries turn a profit. Sister M was a spirited competitor and was resented by some regulars for the advantage of her outfit, but mostly she beat them fair and square.

Of the rest, Easy Ed was the benchmark that any serious devotee measured himself against. Although some of the old-timers thought he had lost a step or two, to see him shamble down the driveway was what it must have been like being in the field when Babe Ruth came to the plate. Easy Ed was a real Hall of Famer, always getting a piece of the ball, likely to turn an improbable offering into a round tripper, and an avuncular assassin on the base paths.

Others, too, had their charm. Lars, heroically proportioned as a WPA post office mural, brooded over his hair in the rear-view mirror before venturing forth. Lars specialized in aquariums and women's clothing.

And the Maldonados. Of indeterminate number, they inhabited a great rusty Oldsmobile with scarcely a memory of shocks or muffler. They would arrive at sales with various appendages and early purchases protruding from trunk and window. After a round of nimble bargaining, the Maldonados returned to the car into which they and their goods disappeared as if into a fairy tale. The Olds was a hard starter in hot or cold weather and seemed to be kept on the road largely through doses of some greenish elixir administered from a container concealed in a Kmart shopping bag. On different occasions, Roger had seen one or another Maldonado pour this tonic into the radiator, the crankcase, the transmission, and the gas tank.

With Amanda gone, Roger had no reason to stay in touch with the neighbors, nor they with him. Without really meaning to, however, Roger broke one of the most sacred of suburban covenants: he neglected his lawn until the Bermuda grass was beyond resurrection. This brought a visit from Tony Merriman, husband of Amanda's best friend among their neighbors. His purpose was to determine how far Roger had declined and whether further slippage could be expected. Roger had not liked him ever since Tony hogged the net in leading his team to an embarrassingly easy victory over Roger's side in a volley-ball match at a neighborhood barbecue some years back. Mimi Merriman was no favorite of Roger's, either. Mimi was a partisan of natural fiber both in food and clothing. She drove an MG that she'd had since college and took private art lessons. Roger had always thought of her as avoidably stupid. He was disappointed that Amanda had imagined them an extracurricular match.

At the door, Tony sniffed around politely, but Roger knew he wouldn't have long to wait; indirection was not Tony's long suit.

"Well, you know, Rog . . ." Tony angled his head sympathetically and rapped the doorjamb crisply with his knuckles. "Sometimes life just throws you a screwball."

Tony was a big Mariners fan, which gave Roger some satisfaction each year as they plummeted towards the cellar for another season. Tony leaned a little to get a better look past Roger into the house.

"Yes," Roger said, nodding across the street where Mimi's MG seemed to graze at the cropped lawn, "but that's no reason to marry it." He smiled sweetly and shut the door.

Sometime after the lawn went under, Roger lost his job. He had been counseled twice about his productivity, so when auditors found he was using mainframe time for personal business, the company let him go. Roger opted for a separation bonus in lieu of six months of Outward Mobility workshops.

Although he missed the money, the job really had become quite a nuisance. Roger had a little something set aside that Amanda's lawyer had not discovered. He calculated that with his unemployment benefits and some judicious resales, he would make out OK. He found it hard to part with any of his acquisitions, but once they were gone he never missed them. Roger didn't have the knack for selling, but he made it a point to pay careful attention so that he rarely received less than he should.

Without the distraction of a job, Roger was able to devote his full attention to the tour. The results were spectacular. Crafty and hardened veterans who ran permanent sales pulled out pieces they had been holding back and cut prices to ruinous levels, as though some gravitational field drew their merchandise to Roger. For his part, Roger bought with a natural grace that left his competitors charmed. Sister Mentholatum had at first been standoffish, suspecting that Roger's new mastery owed something to the black arts. Her fears were allayed, however, when she discovered that he was a lapsed Presbyterian. Sister M's ecumenical experience had taught her that the Devil never bothered with Calvinists of any stripe: he preferred to make God put up with them. Easy Ed hinted that he had been looking for a partner, and the Maldonados made it a point to touch him for luck whenever they brushed past. Only Lars remained unmoved, lugging off his aquariums and pleated skirts in some kind of Nordic funk.

By the end of the summer, Roger was winding up a spectacular season with a dazzling performance in the great sales before the autumn rains. "Mr. October," the Maldonados called him. Ginger, too, when she spoke to him for the first time at a yard sale on Queen Anne Hill.

"Oh, that's just a way of talking, like a nickname." Roger took a reflexive step back from the aurora of auburn hair that flared above her lime green dress.

"I know where the name comes from and I know it fits. To tell the truth, I've been watching you. And asking around."

"How come I didn't—"

"When you're buying, you're so far gone you wouldn't notice Mount St. Helens going off. Listen. Here's the point." Her hair was lit like a torch by the sun. "I want to see it, your collection. I want you to take me home with you."

"Home?"

"Sure. Listen. You're the best; I mean, maybe the best that ever was."

Being picked up like this seemed improbable to Roger, but not unpleasant. He guessed that he ought to be suspicious, but the woman seemed entirely without guile. It was as though his sister had asked to come home with him.

"Who are you?"

"Ginger."

"OK, sure. You want to follow me, or what?"

"I'll just tag along with you."

In the car, Ginger seemed at ease, certainly more so than Roger. She told him a little more about herself, releasing a spicy aroma whenever she shook her hair or recrossed her legs.

"My ex is a dentist; he takes care of the upkeep. I've got some pictures. He'd have to leave town, maybe the state, if they got around. The point is, I pay my own way."

When they arrived, Ginger turned down a drink until after the tour. Roger took her from room to room and through the narrow aisles of the basement. A flush rose up on her as they went, and once or twice she made little excited noises low in her throat. Back in the living room, she faced Roger head-on.

"Magnificent."

"Well, thanks. I don't know, I guess it's more like, maybe, an interest." Roger was grateful that a word arose to complete the sentence.

"Sure. Like drinking's a hobby for an alcoholic. You have the passion for it. I could tell right away and now I'm sure. Jesus, just look around."

"I guess so." Although Roger had always felt a certain affection for his acquisitions, he had trouble imagining that they might arouse stronger passions.

"I guess I still don't see exactly what your interests are."

Ginger shifted her torso and he caught the spicy aroma again. Her hair blazed up in the beige and cream room.

"I look for the best. The world is full of half-cocked washouts, but I found out there's different. Not celebrities. A regular girl's got no chance there. But a little off the beaten track, you'd be surprised. I'm telling you this so we don't have to go into it later on. The first time, it was this guy who won the Grand Sweepstakes three years straight in the Snohomish County Fair leafy vegetable division. He retired the trophy. Jesus, you should have seen his kale."

"Why didn't you, I mean, what happened with him?"

A vague look came into Ginger's face.

"Something to do with fertilizer, I think. Burned up his crop or something." She brightened. "But I caught on with Bobby right away. You know, in a single year he had 167 letters published in papers all over the country. And not one letter the same. I mean, the guy was hot."

"But he cooled off?"

Ginger swung her head in annoyance.

"He got sidetracked by magazines. I don't know why, but he just didn't have whatever it took. He tried to go back to newspapers, but he'd lost the touch."

"Who was next?"

Ginger's expression narrowed. "There's no need to go into all that. I just wanted to give you an idea of my standards so you wouldn't think I was some kind of kook."

"So what happens now?"

"Why, anything you like." Ginger touched him in a way he could not mistake.

Later, in bed, Roger asked if they shouldn't go back to pick up her car.

"No need." Ginger blew out a drowsy cloud of smoke. "I took a cab."

In the morning, Roger woke first. The smell of smoke and bodies was disorienting in the familiar room. Ginger hugged a pillow in sleep, her hair fanned across the sheet like embers. By the time Roger had finished in the bathroom, Ginger was rattling through cupboards in the kitchen. Roger fixed the coffee, then sat at the table while she cooked. She made pasty pancakes blackened at the edge, bacon whose raw ends curled up in despair, and a cottage cheese, egg, and curry compound that brought tears to his eyes and made his fillings ache. This was accompanied by a number of gigantic straw-colored vitamins which Roger declined.

"You keep a pretty good kitchen for a single man. It hardly matters, I'm such a rotten cook. So, can I stay?"

Roger could see that he was going to say yes.

"What would you do?"

"Whatever I want—whatever you want." Her smile was generous; her teeth, a carnivore's. "Like last night."

Sometimes Ginger went along with him. More often, she stayed at home. What she did in either case Roger could not have said. At the sales, Roger bartered and bought submerged in serene attentiveness. He was always a little surprised to find her there when he surfaced with his merchandise. Not once did she urge a particular purchase on him. Her enthusiasm was so general that he could not guess what, if anything, gave her special pleasure.

In March, Roger became aware that Sister Mentholatum no longer appeared at the sales. He asked around, but no one seemed to know anything. Roger thought about calling her order, but he could not recall its name, nor, he realized, did he know her own. One night at supper, he asked Ginger when she had last seen Sister M.

"Our Lady of the Maytag? You can scratch her off."

"Why? What happened?"

"The way I hear it, the old gal was checking out a dryer. She was hauling around a bagful of electrical stuff: toasters, electric razors, radios, hair dryers, alarm clocks. That sort of thing. Anyway, all of a sudden she went off like a slot machine—just lit right up like a jukebox." Ginger flashed her teeth. "She must have looked like Our Lady of Las Vegas before they unplugged her."

"She's dead?"

"Listen, that old penguin was going to cut the heart right out of you. She was all set to expand. She was going to recruit a bunch of junior nuns—stake them out all over the city. It would have finished you."

"How come you know all this?"

"Lover, things come up; I pay attention."

That night, Ginger made love furiously. In the morning, Roger had forgotten something else he'd meant to ask her about Sister M.

The first sign of trouble came not long after. Easy Ed's new partner, a lanky kid with a run of acne and a watch that doubled as a calculator, beat Roger out of a collection of several hundred keys. The same week, Easy Ed started to show up more often on the circuit, and the week after that Roger stayed home one day.

At first, Ginger said nothing. However, she began to go with him more often, and after a young couple took a pewter bedpan almost literally out of his hands, Ginger became a thorny fixture at his side. Things leveled off briefly, but the pros soon found ways to get around Ginger and the slippage continued. At home, she was concerned but upbeat.

"It's just a slump, that's all. Even the great ones can't get it up sometimes. I remember right in the middle of his streak, Bobby got stuck for three weeks on an antivivisection letter."

Ginger made sure he got enough sleep and set him to work pedaling on an exercise bicycle she'd found in the basement. At her insistence, Roger began taking her medley of vitamins. White ridges appeared on his gums and his bowels steamed round the clock like a compost pit. Otherwise, he could detect little change.

As the slump deepened, Ginger took a more forthright approach. The matter reached a crisis when she found him one morning hiding out on the basement toilet, pants around his ankles, reading the sports page. She tore the paper from his hands.

"OK, champ. Enough's enough. I'm not going to just hang around and watch you throw it all away." Ginger cocked a hip. "Remember what it was like when you were out there, when you were the best?"

Roger nodded. He wanted to pull up his pants, but Ginger was standing too close for him to get up.

"And remember what this felt like?" She nipped his thigh between her nails. For the past week, she'd enforced strict celibacy in hopes of fueling his aggressiveness. "Has it ever been this good?"

Roger thought back, but his erotic memory dried up at Amanda. He shook his head no.

"OK, then. What I want you to do is get out there. And when you come back, I want to see that you've turned this thing around. I want to lay my hands on it and know I've got a winner again." She sharpened her gaze. "Got the picture?"

Roger nodded again, his neck already going a little stiff from looking up at her. Her hair flared behind her as she spun away out of the room.

For his part, Roger could no more account for the waning of his talent than he had been able to explain its sudden appearance. Nor had he any particular interest in probing the matter. Ginger had urged him to consult a therapist who specialized in realigning the body's magnetic field. Ginger was certain this polarization therapy had straightened her out after her divorce. So far, however, Roger had managed to sidestep being coated in Vaseline, rolled in iron filings, and strapped down for six hours on top of an electromagnet.

Still, he supposed he really ought to be a good sport and see if he couldn't get the hang of it again. Roger had enjoyed his prosperity on the circuit; Ginger had gormandized on it. He didn't guess any harm could come from taking another crack at it.

He went back to one of his earliest haunts, a stretch of student and pensioner rentals near the university. Several sales were in progress, and Roger moved from one to the next, waiting for the feeling to rise. As he drove the streets, he felt the prick of nostalgia. With his sore neck, he could imagine himself some gimpy ex-slugger, come back to the fields of old glory. He could not, however, imagine himself playing the game again. He thought of getting something for Ginger as a gesture of goodwill, but when he tried to buy a pillbox the man derisively doubled the price and Roger refused to pay it. As he was leaving the sale, he had to shinny off the porch past the Maldonados who were just arriving. The last of the group, perhaps the grandmother of them all, crossed herself and spit in both palms as she passed.

Home, Roger expected the worst, but Ginger was calm, even polite. In bed, she kept stiffly to her side, but Roger's neck was too troublesome for him to undertake any reconciliation.

The next day, Ginger urged him to try again. Prepared for anything except her sweetness, Roger agreed. He drove past a few sales, but could not bring himself to stop. He spent most of the afternoon at a branch library, reading back issues of the *Post-Intelligencer* sports section. Late in the afternoon, he took the long way home.

Roger was most of the way down the block before he realized that the fire truck was parked in front of his house. He was not entirely surprised. The Merrimans were in his driveway talking to a police officer. Mimi detached herself as Roger came up.

"It was that redhead of yours, I'm sure of it. She and that chunky blond. You hadn't been gone ten minutes this morning when they backed up a U-Haul and cleaned you out. Of course, I didn't imagine, I mean at the time, what was going on."

"Of course," Roger said pleasantly. "We all could have been moving to Spokane."

The fire captain came up and said it looked like a cigarette had been left burning on the dresser. The bedroom and garage were total losses, but the rest of the house was only smoke damaged. He took the police officer inside to show him.

"The thing that galls me most," said Mimi, "was to see that side of beef hauling out some of Amanda's old dresses. I mean he was even, you know, holding them up to himself when she wasn't looking."

Amanda had never been exactly svelte, but even at her most robust, Roger did not think that much of her clothing was going to fit Lars.

Two firemen were beginning to uncouple the hoses in the driveway. Mimi and Tony hopped aside to the former lawn. Roger stood still, the sooty water streaming around his shoes.

Tony scuffed his loafer sincerely at the dead turf.

"What will you do now?"

"Go back to Technometrics, I imagine."

"Just like that?" Mimi hooked her fingers under the waistband of Tony's slacks.

Roger looked at his shoes. "Well, I suppose I'll have to get cleaned up."

"No, we mean, well, you've been under a lot of—this must have been . . ." Tony brightened. "You know, Rog, sometimes life just throws you a screwball."

Roger stared at Tony with a gaze so neutral and direct that Tony wondered if Roger had heard him or was perhaps waiting for him to expand on the point. Roger looked away wistfully at the charred and sodden mattress still smoldering in the driveway.

"I'm not sure I was cut out for this."

Mimi's ceramic earrings chimed as she tilted her head. "Cut out for what?"

Roger gestured at the steaming ruins, but his arm swept on to take in the rest of the street and with a rising of his palm the patriarchal towers of the city, oddly rounded at this distance, curving across the horizon like a gathering of Amazons.

Outrider

They approached the high basin from the south, riding single file, three watersheds north of the Staked Plains. The Marshal rode in front, whistling an air from Schubert. Behind him, reins slack in his bandaged hands, came a second man. A little distance back, and just to the right out of the dust drift, the third rider followed, eyes gritted. They circled down to the basin floor and swung into the October sun, through sage, juniper, and chaparral, all afternoon to the western flank of the bowl.

The cabin hardly seemed an artifact. Sod and stone and aspen logs, it looked as though it had simply arisen there. The man had expected adobe. It was his only expectation.

The horses blew and browsed and the wind came up a little. The Marshal waited beside the second man while the deputy remained an edgy distance behind them. Finally, the man with the broken hands got down. The Marshal leaned across and cut free the man's saddlebags and bedroll. The deputy came up then, taking the hanging reins, and the Marshal set down a Winchester in its scabbard and on top of it a gun belt with a long-barreled Colt in the holster. The deputy rearranged his angle in the saddle.

"Keep in touch." The deputy had been waiting to say it all the way out, and the waiting had given it just the edge he wanted.

Long after they were gone, before he entered the cabin, the man flared his head back and sent a seared, stammering howl into the cavity of air far across the basin.

"I'd never go out like that." In his duster, the deputy popped in the wind. He didn't like to make noise, but the weather had turned on them. Already, pellets of sleet buckshot his back. They would camp two nights in the early snow before they got down and south of it.

"No, J. T., you wouldn't."

"I'd sooner go farm or clerk; I'd sooner be blowed the hell

away. No one to go up against. You'd get stale, lose your touch. Even him."

"Out there, he goes against Leit and Corder and Benecelli."

"They're all dead."

"Yes."

The sleet was beginning to rime the deputy's mustache. The Marshal, ruddy and clean-shaven, drew a woolen muffler across his face.

"I expect you got your reasons, but I can't see it. You ask me, I'd say plant him and be shut of it. Or bring him in, like Lever." J. T.'s face was raw and livid as a welt. "Maybe I just don't see the big picture, how it's all supposed to turn out."

"Perhaps we'll get around to that sometime."

"If we have to?"

"If I have to."

The woman had been there two days before the man understood that he had not made her up. He kept her one day after that, and she stayed two more on her own. He had not seen another person in three years. She asked about his work, and he spoke freely. The last night she came at him with a knife as he slept. He caught the little intake of breath as she raised the knife and rolled off the bunk at her legs, still not quite awake, too slow to just knock her down, coming fully awake at the terrible popping of ligaments in her knee. In the morning, she was an hour saddling up, and once mounted could not hold the stirrup with her bad leg.

"And that's all?" The Marshal was massaging oil into the rosewood desk with his palm. "You're quite sure there is nothing else?"

"Quite. His appetites were unnatural, of course. It was more graphic than any fantasy of J. T.'s and as subtle as your history. But I know how pornography bores you."

She leaned into her cane getting up. The Marshal wondered if he should keep using dancers. They were the best athletes he knew of and had done well enough in the past, but they were sticklers for form, always a little rehearsed and self-aware, always beatable by intuition and reflex.

"And his eyes?"

The woman stopped but did not look back.

"Gray. Gray going to agate. Some graininess in the whites in the sun."

When Lever came to see him, the man caught the movement first, far out on the basin floor, and knew it was Lever as soon as he made out his odd gait in the saddle. He and Lever had been close, years ago when they rode together, but they had lost touch except by reputation. Lever rode straight in, and slowly, giving the man plenty of time. He sighted him in the last three hundred yards. Lever came past the stand of aspen whistling, and the man moved out of the trees behind him.

"No need for that," said Lever. He pulled up, unhooked his gun belt, and stepped down, slinging the belt across his saddle.

Instinct, the man thought, or had he made some noise? No, instinct. Lever walked up, his head at an odd angle, as though his neck had been broken.

"Just in the neighborhood and thought I'd see how you were making out. If there was anything I could do. You can put that away. Look here." Lever wiggled his fingers at his eyes. A creamy haze. "Ten, maybe fifteen percent at the sides; straight on it's as black as my heart."

They talked mostly about the old days until all the whiskey Lever had brought was gone. Then Lever talked very carefully about the new days.

"I'm seen to," he said. "You should see my reviews. They made it so easy there's nothing to it, even with these." He thumbed his eyes. "Let me show you."

They went outside with the whiskey bottles. Lever strapped on his gun belt and the man stood behind him, the Colt tucked in his pants.

"Just off either shoulder, any height."

Lever picked the neck off the first, pitched in an easy arc, and shattered the second, a spinner. The third came past him waist-high, fifteen feet out and humming. It exploded at his second shot. And he came on around, in a crouch, head swiveling like a turret, and there was no one there. Lever straightened up and fired his last two shots into the dirt.

"I was always quicker, but you was always smarter."

The man moved out of the cabin; he had stepped back with each toss and had thrown the last bottle from the doorway.

"Go on, then." Lever cartwheeled his pistol as high as the aspen and the man took off the trigger and hammer on the way up.

Lever retrieved the pistol. "Well, then, I guess I'll be getting along. Unless there's something else."

The man shot off both of Lever's index fingers at the second knuckle.

The Marshal had to spend a long time with Lever before he got most of the truth out of him. He had closed the drapes to spare Lever the glare from the courtyard. He liked the husky light in the room, and left them drawn when the sun passed from the courtyard.

"How the hell am I going to get along with these?" Lever splayed his hands on the desk, smudging the finish. The Marshal sighed. Lever disappointed him.

"With mechanical aids, or a ghostgunner; perhaps a *doppelgänger*. You may count on our support as long as you do nothing embarrassing. Understand, however, that the main circuit is now out of the question."

"You bastards. What if I told the truth?"

The rasping swish of clippers sheared the air in the room as the gardener pruned the boxwood back. The Marshal sat still in the dead center of Lever's vision.

"I was just talking; I mean, I'm pretty worked up, that's all."

"Yes. You were going to tell me about his eyes."

"Well, I did the best I could. Pig iron, I'd say."

"And the whites?"

"Clear. Oh, Jesus, I haven't seen any that bright since Sammy Shaniko."

Lever started to cry, a sort of jerky hiccuping that he tried to talk through. At times like these, the Marshal was sure he should have gone into banking.

"He can be got, Marshal, I swear it. It took him four shots to pick my pistol apart. I looked it all over. He missed it clean twice. Let J. T. at him; J. T. could take him out."

When Lever was gone, the Marshal lit the lamps and wiped down his desk. J. T. might indeed be able to do it; he certainly wanted to do it, even after riding ahead of Lever and working his way down the rim with glasses. Of his four shots, the man had fired the first two into the dirt. J. T. was good, but the Marshal couldn't risk it. A man as fast and mean and stupid as J. T. was not a prize to squander. They still turned them out mean and stupid, but fast was a gift. It could not be arranged.

They went back in July, under an operatic sky. The Marshal had hoped for Wagnerian weather, had waited for it six weeks once he made up his mind. The spectral cumulus and prismatic sunsets exceeded his expectations. J. T. was bileful. The Marshal had been firm about his part in it. He had bought one day of silence by seeing to it that J. T. set out with a glacial hangover; he got two more days of sulk. He could manage two days of talk.

"I'd let him rot. I'm telling you, if it was up to me I'd leave it the hell alone. Not that it's much of a chance after all this time. If he was coming back, he'd come by now. Not a word in years. Why mess with it?"

"Because he didn't quit or change."

"How the hell do you know?"

"I have made it a point to know what I needed to."

"What finally gets to them in the end? Money, pussy, a big name? Just wearing out?"

"Yes. Also, they respect me."

J. T. broke a raw laugh. "They hate your guts."

"That too."

"What about him?"

"I'm not certain yet."

"I thought you knew everything."

"If this didn't take some discretion, any shootist could do it."

"Even me, I suppose."

"I suppose."

The fifth day out, coming into the chalk hills that marked the edge of the basin, they flushed a band of ravens that detonated from a carcass in the brush, spooking the horses. The riderless roan broke away, and they lost six miles running him down. It also cost them the sun, and they made camp early, waiting for morning. The Marshal wanted to go in with the sun low and at his back.

"Have I ever told you, J. T., that you are without peer in healing berserkers?" The Marshal dropped in an extra measure of coffee and chicory for the pot.

"Nobody ever had to. I never seen anybody handle them any better."

"Yes, they are best dealt with among us, and directly. But I must tell you that berserkers hold little interest for me anymore; I am grateful that I can trust them to you. But the others—few enough, *bien entendu*—the ones that cannot be healed, gone into the weather, the outriders, J. T. . . . . "

The deputy was bored.

"How many you figure you brought back?"

The Marshal settled the pot into the coals. He had been talking to himself again. He would have to see that cellist when they got back.

"As many as I had to."

The Marshal left J. T. on the rim with glasses. He was to come in only after it was over, or if something went wrong. The Marshal led the horses down and was well out on the basin floor by first light. Whenever he was away from the basin, he used it as the measure of earthworks, yet when he was in it he saw how little it left to the imagination. There was probably an article for someone in that.

As he approached the stand of aspen, the Marshal saw that the man had stripped bark from the trunks and main limbs. He had been careful not to disturb the inner bark; not all of them had been such attentive botanists. If the aspen were not so prolific, the residents so few, the grove would have been gone by now. The Marshal was certain the man was not in the grove, but he was almost as sure he was not in the cabin. The scrolls of aspen were stretched on a lattice of drying racks to the side of the cabin. The Marshal aimed his horse towards them, stopping forty feet out.

"I've come alone." A mistake. The tinny taste came up in his mouth. "I left J. T. on the rim; there is no one else."

The Marshal leaned forward in the saddle and rubbed at a bulge along his horse's jawline. The gelding gummed at the bit, raising a knot of muscles the Marshal had to unravel each night.

The man emerged then from the drying racks, hands like jewelers' scales, balancing his carbine. He moved laterally until the cabin was at his back. The roan sidestepped prissily, swinging out until the tether to the gelding snapped his head around.

"Things have changed," said the Marshal. "You are needed."

The man gestured and the Marshal dropped his gun belt and rifle; the man motioned again, the carbine moving with the elegance and precision of a baton, and the Marshal unsnapped his cuffs and rolled both sleeves above his elbows. He had an awkward time with his boots, but finally managed to wedge them in the stirrups and work his feet out.

"A completely free hand," said the Marshal. "No interference, no adjustments, on whatever terms you name. You have my absolute word."

Behind an Old Testament beard, the man's mouth gave away nothing, but his eyes came unmuzzled and the Marshal fixed them in his memory. They were entire beyond all reckoning.

And the man slackened the Winchester and poured his chest into a rising pillar of triumph and the Marshal stretched again to rub at the gelding's knot and the horse's head leaned aside into the rubbing and with his other hand under the mane, in the pouch sutured to the roots of the mane, he arranged the ivory derringer and moving the gelding a fraction with his knees shot the man very carefully through the throat.

The Marshal tied the horses in the grove. He could see the dust scrawled out behind J. T. as he came headlong down the flank of the bowl. The Marshal walked back to the body. Already, flies had begun to browse the wound. He squatted down. The eyes were almost gone, but as he watched they fissured deep, then filled with sludge.

The Marshal was finishing his inventory when J. T. arrived. J. T. examined the body and grunted his professional admiration.

"You are still one son of a bitch to be reckoned with." Blood made J. T. careless. The Marshal looked up from the scrolls. He had an unflinching respect for certain profanity; it brought bad luck. His analyst, so helpful in other matters, had been unable to dowse the source of this. J. T. had trouble sometimes with the proscribed phrases.

"I mean, Marshal." J. T. didn't like to back up. "I saw him in San Saba once. I was just a kid, but I knew what to look for. He couldn't have got any quicker since. I could have taken him head on."

The Marshal thought about the eyes.

"No."

"What happens now?"

J. T. had gotten the man up on the roan with some trouble, and though the man sat the horse awkwardly, he would limber up on the ride back. By the time they reached town he would be perfectly at ease, indistinguishable.

"We will absorb him, and sanctify him."

The Marshal's hand was stiff from taking notes. Perhaps J. T. could learn photography. The Marshal heaped all the bark from the cabin around the drying racks. He folded away a sonnet-sized piece and set the pile afire.

"Sanctify?"

"J. T., you had better learn language before your reflexes go. It means to make holy."

"I'd say you made a fair start with that derringer. I still don't see what's so special about him now."

"He will acquire a reputation. And we are safe."

"From him?"

"From ourselves, which have always been plain to him."

"Well why the hell didn't we just get it over with back then? We got better things to do than run around the country like missionaries. It ain't efficient."

"He had to be verified for those who notice such things. That could not have happened among us. He has been etched; now we will ink him with fame. He becomes a reproduction, a recitation."

"Hadn't we ought to shave him? So folks will know who he is?"

J. T. didn't like it. The berserkers were rabid, but that was different. This one looked like a dreaming loony, a Hutterite.

The kind you went after with dogs and a picnic lunch. J. T. was scrupulous about several things. He never backshot a man unless he had to, and he left the feebleheaded to the preachers' bountymen.

"It is the mark of wilderness on him, the authentic sign that he is not ours."

"Is he? He ain't much, for sure, but the son of a bitch, I mean, he is still strange. How do you know?"

"I have a strict obligation never to mistake such men. Call it a touch, my gift. A tint, a gesture, an inflection—they assemble themselves into certainty." The Marshal stopped, savored. He felt the shiver of pleasure, almost sexual, at rubbing words together until they came. He also knew that it angered and frightened J. T. He relaxed his grip.

"The way, say, you know a man is going to draw before he knows it himself; who, among strangers, you must always keep in sight on a street; when the tree line conceals an ambush and the moment to break for cover."

"That's just good sense."

"Yes, and you are well rewarded for it."

"I'm alive."

"I suppose."

"Well, it's more than this asshole." He drew and spun off four slugs, then a fifth, exploding the pulpy spine of a yucca. "You think he's something better than me. Like you'd like to throw in with him."

"That is why I am proficient."

They came into town mid-afternoon, the sky almond at their backs, a big blow on the way behind them from the Staked Plains. The Marshal's clerk met them at the ford. There was money at the bank in the man's name; two women lay coiled in bed in his suite at the hotel. The citizens mostly went about their business, but a few spoke and the Marshal returned their greetings by name. As they passed the hotel on their way to the livery, the Marshal was gratified at the number of brokers from the academies, ateliers, and foundations. The porch rail was festooned with their prospectuses. A scout from the Prize and Bounty Consortium lounged in disguise at the hotel bar. At an upper window, an envoy from the Chancellery slanted a specimen bottle into the light.

And the man drew himself up, hesitant until the gesture came, then graceful, nodding left and right like a king.

Gospel Hump

This happened to me when I was twenty-one, the summer before my last year of school. I don't know exactly why, but it turned out to be one of those things that keeps cropping up every now and then in your memory.

My life has been pretty ordinary. Some ups and downs, a few surprises, but about what I expected. I was working that summer for the Forest Service as a wilderness ranger. I'd fished and hunted the country north of the Salmon since I was a kid, so I knew the area pretty well. I'd never thought of working there, but I was poking around for a summer job and Dad was in Rotary with the Nez Perce Forest Supervisor and things just fell together.

I'd spend two weeks at a crack patrolling the Gospel Hump Wilderness Area, checking permits, giving directions and advice, putting out campfires—just generally making myself useful. People were usually glad to see me, but some came out for the peace and quiet. Folks like that I tried to leave to themselves.

The incident I mentioned must have happened in early July, because the snow was just off Dolbrow Meadows and the huckleberries were coming on. Dolbrow Meadows is medium wilderness: fifteen miles or so from the trailhead, uphill all the way, and a couple of miles off any trail on the government maps. You have to work some to get there. I'd usually swing over and check it out on my loop through the Maiden Lakes Basin. Now and then somebody would be set up in there. If no one was around, I'd stay the night myself. The mosquitoes were never bad, and the meadow gave you a great view of Three Fingered Jack. I guess I haven't been back through since Dad and I went elk hunting the year he died.

I don't know when I'd thought of it last, but I never expected the whole memory to just walk into my office. The woman was in her late fifties, a well-dressed, no-nonsense sort. She wanted to buy some five-year renewable term. She'd already filled out the forms with Cynthia and had taken a physical so we got right down to business. I ran through the options, but she seemed to know what she wanted so I went ahead and filled out the contract. Her beneficiary was a woman living at the same address. When I asked the nature of their relationship, she wanted to know if that was on the form. I said it was, and she said "friend." While I was wrapping everything up, she sat looking at me in a way that made me feel off-balance.

"You don't remember me, of course."

I reran the name, Sheila Held, but she was right. Dad could never understand how I get by in the business when I don't keep track of people any better than I do.

"I have more reason to remember you. Twenty-three years ago you helped me out of the woods."

And then, of course, it came back.

"Dolbrow Meadows."

"What?"

"The woman in the tent."

"Yes."

I'd seen the tent before I broke out of the timber into the meadow, and my day got a little worse. Some yellow jackets had nailed me that morning, and the Tangent Butte lookout had relayed a message that my boss wanted me to come out two days early for a driver safety workshop. Now I'd have to go on another hour to set up for the night. Nobody who camped this far off the beaten track wanted any company. At least whoever was there—if they were even around—wouldn't likely want to chat. I could just show the flag and shove off.

Nobody was outside the tent, so I struck up a tune when I hit the meadow. I liked to let people know I was coming, so I'd whistle on the way in if I couldn't see anyone at a campsite, especially if there was a tent. You never know.

As I got closer, I could hear something coming from the tent, and then I could tell it was a woman crying. I pulled up and just stood there, maybe a hundred feet off. The tent flap was closed so I couldn't see anything, but the crying didn't sound like it was going to stop and from the gear outside it looked like it was only one person. I went ahead and hollered hello. The crying stopped, and the second time I hollered the woman unzipped the flap and stuck her head out.

"U.S. Forest Service, ma'am. Is everything all right?" Our green and khaki uniforms didn't exactly stand out, and you couldn't really make out the badge or name tag until I got up pretty close.

"I'm a wilderness ranger. Gary Shadling. Can I help out, ma'am?"

"Don't call me ma'am. I'm not a schoolteacher, and I'm not eighty years old."

"Sorry."

"Well, what do you want?"

"I'm a U.S. Forest Service wilderness ranger—"

"Yes, I believe we've established that."

"Well, I guess I just wanted to be sure everything was all right."

"Do you make a point of dropping in on people to see how their lives are going?"

"Most people aren't crying in their tent."

"No, I wouldn't think so." All the time she was looking at me in the kind of neutral and direct way men have of sizing each other up. It looked like she'd been crying for a while.

"So is there anything else? Can you just ranger on out of here?"

"I guess I could do that. I need to see your permit first."

"Permit."

"Wilderness permit. They're in a box at the trailhead."

"I don't have one."

"The Forest Service requires a permit for wilderness use."

"My partner had it. Are you going to arrest me?"

"When your partner comes back, tell him that we like people to leave their permits at camp."

"I'll be sure to pass that information on."

"Fine." I hitched my pack around on my shoulders and started out into the meadow.

"Wait. Did you see a woman, maybe in the last couple of hours? Blonde, athletic-looking. She would have had a white dog with her."

"Yes."

"Which way was she going?"

"Down."

"You mean away from here?"

"Yes."

"Did she say anything?"

"Not much more than hello. She wanted to know if there was a quicker way out."

The woman put the tip of her finger into her mouth as if to bite her nail, then pulled it away.

"Could you form an estimate of her character? Did she seem like the sort of person who would bring someone out into the middle of nowhere and then carve them up for dead? No, never mind. Go on. Go. Just go."

She went into the tent and zipped herself in. I waited to see if she was going to cry again. She didn't, so I went on across the meadow. When I reached the timber, I looked back. Even from that distance, I could see the tent sagging on one side where it hadn't been staked right. I went on back.

When I got within range, I could hear her crying, rougher this time. I called out, and when she didn't respond I walked up near the tent.

"I just wanted to let you know I'm going to be setting up for the night across the way here."

Her voice came out strangled. "I'm not crazy. Leave me alone. I'm OK. I'm just hurt."

"It's too late for me to go on. I'll stay out of your way. Just give me a yell if you need anything."

I pitched my tent within earshot and cooked supper on my campstove. Somewhere in there she stopped crying. The quiet was almost as bad. I washed up and made my log entry for the day propped up against my pack, watching the sunset light up the snow on the north ridge of Three Fingered Jack.

It was late dusk when she started rustling around in the tent. A flashlight came on, and after some more rummaging and swearing she came out.

"Do you have any toilet paper?"

"Sure."

I got a roll out of my pack and met her halfway. She headed towards the timber, walking stiffly and carefully. It was dark when she came back.

"Thanks."

"I'm going out tomorrow; go ahead and keep it."

"My friend had most of that stuff in her pack."

"She's the one I passed?"

"Yes."

"Never go without a spare."

"Partners or toilet paper?"

I laughed. "I don't know about partners."

"Mine seem to think they have a lot in common with toilet paper. Why don't you have a fire?"

I explained to her that meadows were delicate. A fire ring scarred the sod for a long time.

"You wouldn't have some coffee?"

"How about something to eat?"

"No, just coffee, thanks."

She sat down while I lit the stove and boiled up some water.

"It's just instant."

"Fine."

The silences didn't feel comfortable, but they weren't too bad.

"You weren't aiming to come here, were you?"

"No. Janet heard about a lake. Some body part—tongue, elbow . . . "

"Finger."

"That's it."

"You're a little off track."

"I'll bet I am. I don't even really know my way out of here."

"You parked at the Maiden Lakes trailhead?"

"Where you come up from Boise?"

"Yes."

"I guess that's it."

"I can walk you out in the morning if you want."

"Thank you."

We drank the coffee and she had a second cup. Most people seem to expand or shrink in the dark. She stayed about the same.

"What's the worst thing that ever happened to you?"

"I'm not sure anything like that ever has." I thought about it. "Maybe when my granddad died."

"Are you going to ask me?"

"No," I said, "I don't think so."

We sat a while longer. Once or twice I thought we were going to talk some more, but we didn't. After a while, she said good night and went back to her tent.

I woke up fast in the morning, the sour smell of bad smoke in my nose—not wood smoke, but an acid, plastic smell. The woman was standing next to a smudgy little fire, poking at her sleeping bag with a stick. The bag wasn't burning very well, and the smoke hung across the meadow in the heavy morning air. I got my jeans on and went over.

"I'm sorry about the mess. I'll send the Sierra Club a check when I get home."

I came back from the timber with a load of wood and stoked up the fire. I didn't tell her that burning plastic gave off toxins that were bad news for everybody, especially birds. I didn't expect she'd be doing that again.

After breakfast I struck my tent and packed up. She came back from the timber and started getting her things together. Her clothes were expensive—Eddie Bauer kind of stuff—but her trail gear was pretty flimsy. She wanted to leave the tent, but I said we'd have to pack it out.

We started to drop the tent when she remembered that they'd brought in some large rocks to anchor it along one side where they couldn't get the stakes to hold. I crawled in and started tossing the rocks out. The last one at the back of the tent was flat on top. There was a pile of capsules on it and a prescription bottle. I scooped the pills into my hand and pitched the rock out front. Back out, I gave her the bottle and held out my hand with the capsules. They had gone a little soggy in the night air and were stuck together. Some of the color came off on my palm.

"These probably won't do you any good now."

"No," she said, giving me another direct look and taking a step back. "I won't be needing them."

I dumped the pills into what was left of the fire where they made a damp little hiss. I shook out some water from my canteen and stirred the embers with my trail shovel. I doused them again and then felt around with my hand.

"Isn't that overdoing it? I couldn't get that going again if my life depended on it."

"You never know for sure till you feel around. You don't want it coming back on you."

We made good time going out. The woman's boots were giving her some trouble, but I let her set the pace when we hit the trail and she trucked right along. We took a break at the Sharps Creek crossing and had some nuts and raisins.

When we finished, I helped her with her pack and shrugged mine on. We were at most an easy hour out from the trailhead.

"Do you think I'm attractive?"

I fumbled with the cinch on my waist strap bringing it around.

"Well, sure, I guess so. I never really thought about it for a woman your age."

She laughed. "How old do you think I am?"

"Forty?"

"Ouch."

At the trailhead, she thanked me and we shook hands. Her car almost wouldn't start, but then it did and she drove away.

"You saved my life, you know."

She was standing now, snugging the belt on her trench coat.

"How?"

"I don't know, exactly. Coming back when you didn't have to." She tugged the belt into place. "I don't suppose that's something I should be telling someone I just bought life insurance from."

"That was a long time ago."

"Did anything like that ever happen to you again?"

"No," I said.

"Not to me, either."

We shook hands and I walked her to the door.

"What about that name?"

"Which?"

"Gospel Hump. I've always wondered."

"They got it from a couple of mountains in there, Gospel Peak and Buffalo Hump. We used to joke about it when I was in school, but it doesn't mean anything. It's just a name."

Not too long after that she left Spokane. I was still the agent of record, so I handled the paperwork a few years later when she was killed in a car wreck. I thought about writing her beneficiary, but when I checked the file it turned out that she'd changed beneficiaries twice since she took out the policy so I decided I'd better just leave it alone.

Fire Season

I think it is fitting, even, perhaps, necessary, that as I begin this, rain has begun to fall. A simple rain, unaccompanied by wind, without thunder. It will pass, east to the desert, the smell of a new season riding the air till morning. Beneath the rain, the old discontinuities: San Andreas, Santa Sangre, Soledad, Lytle Creek—shape-shifters wound deep, continents in transit on either side. Above the fault lines, green is coming in; this week the yucca will be blooming.

It has been a long time, thirty years almost. Montana, Oregon, Colorado. Grazing rights, timber rights, water rights. I defend the land from its people, and sometimes, arrogant, defend the land even from itself. Thirty years. Time from which I have won a wife, three daughters, and the right to address the Rotary in the name of the Forest Service. I have multiplied my Civil Service rating, learning to manipulate staffs and budgets as fluently as I once swung a brush hook. And now I have come back, at the beginning of another summer, to where I began. Catlow District, Santa Sangre National Forest, full circle. It is a strange thing, such a symmetry.

I am not especially liked by other rangers. Defunct English major, I came to forestry after starting out with books. I read them still: biographies, novels, philosophy, even poetry. This is considered odd and I do not talk much about it. At small, remote ranger stations your life is a party line; word gets around.

Tonight I am moving into the office of the last district ranger. Oscar Steenbergen. Twenty-seven years on the Catlow. Like heroes, district rangers once came large. Although Oscar could not have been more than five-six, no one ever thought him small. I think, even, that Oscar drew assurance from his size. He told me once he liked to think he was closer to the ground that way. In the years I knew him, he never gave me reason to doubt that. Oscar Steenbergen, tending the district like a farm generations in his family. Oscar Steenbergen, his district, now mine. God spare me one half his love and rigor.

59

Rigor. Summer. The first week of my first season. Dalton Hotshots.

"Dalton has never lost a line. Not one. It takes men to do something like that. You measure a man against a fire, you find out what he's put together with. Twenty hours on the line, no food, out of water, snot baked in your nose like a brick, eyes shot from the smoke, cramped up and swearing you'll never do this again as long as you live—that's when you find out who has it and how much of it he's got. You sign on with Dalton, you sign on with the Marines of the Santa Sangre. Anybody who sticks is going to make it because he learned one thing—he learned how to hate fire like you hate a man."

Bob Cable, foreman. In Korea he dragged himself through three hundred yards of snow and got the machine gun that was killing his squad. It cost him some of his body along the way. That kind of man.

The first week of the first season. We started with twenty-nine, trained at the Benbow Station. Each night, there were fewer cars in the compound. Some men were not physical, others inept with tools, and one, massively strong, was too cumbersome to scale the ridges. Those who splintered under Cable's harrowing went too. And he pressured us all, crowding us against the time when buckling would mean losing a line:

"Cavenaugh, you don't chop with a hook. You want to hack on something, go find a Boy Scout hatchet. Slice with it. Slice!"

"Perez, get Pitkin up on your back there, boy, and see if you can't get up the hill and back before I finish my coffee."

"Jarvis, you're a college boy. How long does it take sixteen men to cut a hundred chains of line in medium bitterbrush and light chamise?"

"Orem, it's not the gun, it's the gunner. I can't make a turkey sandwich out of chicken shit."

Cable carved the week out and it seemed, in turn, a decathlon, fraternity initiation, boot camp. Whatever its models, the week made the first raw, decisive strokes that would shape us finally into Cable's own implement—the Dalton Hotshots.

Near the end of the week, I was sharpening shovels and McClouds while Jimmy Graystart worked the brush hooks. I was doing again what I had done wrong all morning. The shovels were dull and the bevel on the McClouds was uneven. New to the crew and the work, I needed to talk, ask questions. I forced them against Jimmy's responses which were more riddle than answer, slanting off from what you wanted to know, often leaving you with a harder question.

He did explain one thing as the afternoon ran down. I had admired his belt buckle, the whole belt really. The leather was tooled in the stylized shape of a man. The buckle, silver and turquoise worked in the figure of an eagle, formed the man's stomach. Jimmy said it was a singer's belt, but it didn't mean anything now because the singers had lost the god-chants and the people no longer listened.

Just before quitting time, a government pickup, shrouded in dust, bounced into the compound and stopped near the tool-shed. The passenger, in immaculate work clothes, got out first. As he came around the truck into full view, I was struck by his face. One side, the left, its flesh drawn tight, had a sort of waxy luminescence, pale as frosted glass. Even with that, the man had one of those neutral faces that take shape in the mid-twenties and remain fixed for another ten or fifteen years. Without the flawed side, he would have been either bland or pretty.

He stood by the truck while Oscar got some papers from the visor. Oscar said hello and asked about Cable. Jimmy said he was in the office, but he wasn't looking at Oscar as he spoke. Holding a hook, he watched the other man whose presence, even under the weight of Jimmy's gaze, was that of one who had answered for himself any question the world could put to him. Oscar said he'd be joining the crew. His name was Martin Speyer, and he'd worked for the Forest Service before on the Mendocino. While I was shaking hands, Jimmy broke off the stare, put down his hook, and said he would get Cable. Speyer watched him go, squinting into the light. Oscar said it was all right, that Jimmy didn't take to people right away. I knew this was true, but it didn't seem true enough. Jimmy's gaze was guarded but deep, and his eyes had gone ugly.

Jimmy Graystart—part Indian, part Mexican, second hook behind Cable. No one could say how old he was. I don't really think he knew himself. He resembled one of those muscular pines, aging against the wind and snow near timberline. He had come out in the forties with the New Mexico Indian crews the government brought west for a few summers. These men, establishing the Dalton legend in the Santa Sangres against long racial odds, had never lost a line. And they had rarely lost a fight. In the end, the Forest Service could no longer justify the weekly rodeo: reclaiming the crew from city and county jails; waiting out three-day poker games in Riverside, three-day drunks in El Monte. One season a bus took them away in October and they never came back. Jimmy was all that remained of that history and his presence pointed back to legends, beginnings from which, as a crew, we once had come.

By the time Speyer had been on the crew a week, he was cutting third hook behind Cable and Jimmy. He was respected, and he was liked. I think he was the most gentle man I have ever known. He found a blue lizard and taught it to run up his arm for shreds of bacon on his shoulder. He named it Milt and could put it in a trance by stroking its belly. One morning we found it slit open, its guts spread out triangular on a rock. That day, cutting practice line, Jimmy missed his footing and stumbled back into Speyer. Jimmy jumped away electrically and spun, pointing his hook. Speyer watched him evenly. Jimmy said something quickly, in Spanish I thought, and turned back to work. Speyer made a small gesture of puzzlement at me and began cutting again.

That evening I sat with Jimmy while he worked grease into his boots. To the northwest, the high domes of the Santa Sangres still held the sun. It was the kind of time you either said nothing at all or talked about important things. I wanted to ask Jimmy about Speyer and finally I did.

After a while he said, "I know him."

"Know him, Speyer? From where?"

"I know him," he said, and touched his buckle with the palm of his hand. "Here."

He began to relace his boots.

"What did you say on the line today? To Speyer?"

"That I had no wish to run into him."

From the beginning Jimmy hated Speyer, beyond reason and without explanation. I have seen hate since, but it has always been able, even eager, to explain itself. Jimmy would say nothing about it at first; later, his references to Speyer were so oblique and fantastic that I could never be certain it was Speyer he spoke of.

Hate that roots like that in a man can rupture a crew. Piece by piece, sides are chosen and each man withdraws to the private circle he stepped out of to form the larger perimeter of the crew. Jimmy's hate, unrelieved, would have broken Dalton. Maybe Cable could have stopped it, but I don't think so.

But before that could happen, summer finished kindling and came in hard. The hills went tinder brown and the burning index was critical. At the end of the week, we had our first roll.

For five weeks we rolled almost every day we weren't already on the line. The low and middle canyons of the Santa Sangres no longer filled with early haze that dissolved in the sun. In its place, ochre smoke stung in the air, the sun a swollen lobe behind it. We came to measure time by shifts, distance in chains of line, and counted as pleasure anything that didn't hurt. Green Peter, Cripple, Arroyo Seco, Ten Mile, Walker Mountain. Three hotshot crews and too much fire. Violin Canyon, Rib Ridge, Schoolhouse, Cargo Creek. They brought in men. Recruits from Fort Ord who complained of the heat, drank too much water, and cramped on the line. Convicts who worked as hard as men paid forty cents an hour are likely to. Pickup crews from the field towns of the San Joaquin Valley who hid in the brush, drank Tokay, broke their tools, and slept. Rincon, Captain Prairie, Rebel Rock. We learned to cut line, balanced on the fatal edge of fatigue. We cut while sweat turned the dust on our faces to mud and wore calluses over our blisters. Dirty, brutal, deadly work.

I learned about fire in those weeks. How a yucca base would burn through and bound down a slope, strewing embers across your line. The way a slope could preheat, the vapors driven from its oily brush, and explode with the sound of a jet lifting off and heat you could feel half a mile away. I watched rabbits, their fur ablaze, in a blind death dash away from the fire. Fire that quit when it had no reason to and burned against all odds; fire that took only ground cover, then wheeled back through the scorched canopy like wind through barbed wire.

July passed and half of August. From Jimmy I learned the small things that help hold a man together on the line. Only the very strongest can muscle their way through; Jimmy showed me how to compensate with technique. I learned to wear two pair of socks and carry extra gloves inside my shirt. I stopped using the vulnerable bow, cinching my boots instead with a double square knot. I had tried gum, sour candy, rocks, anything to suck against thirst. We carried two quart canteens on our pistol belt to replace what we sweated, not to indulge thirst. Jimmy taught me how bitterbrush leaves moistened cottonmouth, the trick of mouthing water and spitting it back in the canteen, and best, the quenching of green oranges.

From Speyer I learned other things. He asked if I'd read *Moby-Dick* and spoke of Bob as our Ahab. He said that fire was the oldest element, that the spirit of man was of fire, and that he had come here, now, to be close to the source of his being. And he smiled and said he read poetry and was not to be believed about such things.

The third week in August the fires stopped. We had held the largest to less than six hundred acres. Cable seemed satisfied that we had tempered into a crew; we, too, felt tough and confident. We had matured with the season, were more than its match. Cable must have known the summer could still erupt beyond anything we had yet cut against. I suppose Speyer and maybe a few others did too. But it was only Jimmy, wedging himself against our poise, whose presence suggested that what had passed was preface.

By the end of August the mountains still ached with heat, but the fire didn't come. We rested, then grew tight again with the waiting. I remember feeling like the way you tense your face before coming around a corner into the wind.

Time slowed and strung itself out, especially after supper. We played poker and pinochle until everybody seemed to run out of money. Some of the crew arm-wrestled or tried to beat Bob at one-arm push-ups. Speyer stayed by himself pretty much, but once he did a trick with a wooden match that was really something. He struck it on the bad side of his face, then somehow bent the flame until it was almost horizontal and made it follow his finger around in a circle, the upper yellow of the flame deepening toward red as it moved. He never showed us how he did it.

And sometimes, late, I listened to uneasy talk of the Santa Ana, the September wind that blew in hot and black from the desert at seventy miles an hour. Stories of thousands of acres lost in a shift and of crews burned. It was called the black angel of the Sangre, for it carried dust and death.

Some of those evenings I spent with Speyer. We'd walk in the late light, out through the hooded scrub oaks beyond the obstacle course. He spoke easily and I liked to listen, liked the sound of his voice drifting quietly into me. He seemed gently sure of things, something I had never seen in a man and never have since. One night I asked him about his face. He said that when he was younger, before he understood about fire, he had made a mistake and was burned.

Jimmy had stopped coming to meals. He waited out the evenings apart, sanding and waxing the handle of his hook, massaging the blade with oil and a whetstone. I sat with him one night and asked about other seasons and about what was going to happen now. When he finally answered, his voice was high, rapid, old, and the words were more Indian than English. What I could understand burned into me and the memory of them, even now, touches a shudder centered somewhere deeper than my bones.

"The smell of him. Fire cunning, death cunning. The man is nothing, a trick. Smell the fire. He waits in the desert and speaks with the devils. Already his doom runners come before him. Whose name cannot be said prepares the way. I am not hands-empty of weapons, but I must gather the luck of all my person against what comes. I cannot help you now. Now, you cannot help me. Make yourself small and close to the earth—a chip of rock, a bead of air, the beetle's underside. Do not be looked for."

I understood then that he was an old man, flickering on the borders of sanity. It was the last time I ever talked to Jimmy.

On the fifth of September, the Forest Service went on Santa Ana alert. After that, we slept in our clothes. On the sixth, it came out of the desert, finding the high passes, accelerating down the slopes and canyons, pouring out across the coastal plain, topography upping the voltage beyond where measurements mean anything. We rolled on the eighth.

The fire was on the Catlow and we hit the line in twenty minutes. By then it was thirty acres, powerful and violent and running with the wind. We started cutting about three and tied off our sector by ten the next morning. In fire camp they told us that a pickup crew had refused to work and the whole west flank, our flank, had been lost. The fire was called Devil's Backbone and had already taken more than three thousand acres.

We ate, then slept until late afternoon. Oscar came to see us before we headed out. He moved and spoke like a man in pain—his district, his crew, his fire. Technically, he was not in charge. In every other way, it was his. In Washington, the statistics on Backbone would be microscopic entries on a computer disk. For Oscar, the losses were inscribed on the raw tissue of memory.

He told us how things stood: four thousand acres, give or take, no estimate of containment; the Santa Ana continuing at least through tomorrow; the Region spread thin trying to cover other fires. He told us tonight could make a difference of ten thousand acres—habitat, watershed, living country. He said he had argued us into a sector where it mattered most, where he would hesitate sending any other crew. And he said it was going to be bad.

Our sector lay along the crest of one of the rib ridges of the Devil's Backbone, striking down, perpendicular, toward the valley. The ridge fell away sharply on both sides and was rooted with a heavy growth of chamise and manzanita, broken here and there by rock croppings and thinning where the brush shaded into the bulk of the Backbone. Our night's work would begin as far up the ridge as a cat skinner could push his machine.

We waited while Cable talked with the skinner. As the dusk took hold we could see, across two miles to the east, the line of the next ridge standing out against the level glow of the fire working its back slope. To the north, odd, evening cumulus had begun to lumber up somewhere beyond the Backbone, out over the desert face of the Santa Sangres. Away from the drift of the diesel fumes, the oil from the brush gave off an acid, urine smell, as though some great beast had marked its territory here.

Cable laid it out for us. We were looking at a mile and a half of cutting, extending the line up the ridge and tying it in to a mammoth rockslide on the western flank of the Backbone. At the first drop in the wind, they would backfire, trying to funnel everything down to where the tankers waited.

We swung into the work, centered on the ridge's axis; balanced between the light feathering out of the sky in the west, the rising illumination of fire to the east. Working out the stiffness, we settled into our rhythm, a purposeful trance of motion that held fatigue in suspension. Bob set the pace at lead hook. Tonight he went out fast, sealed in the rhythm, pushing hard. Behind him, Jimmy hooked in counterpoint, hermetic, submerged beneath our common trance. Speyer seemed less easy than before. I had an odd sense of him ranging outside the cadence: intense, alert, aware beyond the precise wedging arc of his hook. I threw the brush they cut, and, as night settled, the world was bound within our narrow track through the brushfield, the pale circle of light from my headlamp. Beyond that rim, the even dark closed around the brush I hurled into it.

We took our first break around midnight. When the tools had been sharpened, we sat with our headlamps out: smoking, drinking a little water, not saying much, watching. The fire had come over the ridge to the east and was working its flank, tacking down laterally across the wind, filaments of flame raveling the slope. Nearly opposite us, it reached a bench and made a fingering run. Small eddies of paler fire plumed up, spun above the bank of flames, and disappeared. Fire spores carried downwind, infecting the brushfield. A prodigious dance of fire, extravagantly choreographed by fuel, slope, and wind. And above the blowing of the Santa Ana, across nearly a mile, we listened to the steady mammoth roar of its coming.

Although the fire was below us, the wind was our margin of safety, bearing the main firefront away downcanyon. The fire still seeped diagonally down the slope, but it absorbed distance so slowly I could hardly measure its progress. Before the break, I had noticed the brush thinning out a little. Ahead, I could make out the Backbone, opaque against the fainter dark of the sky. I guessed one, maybe two hours, and we'd tie in at the top. I hoped the wind would drop before our shift was over. I wanted to backfire from our line, setting the scorpion against itself. Turning away, we embedded ourselves in the trance of the work that remained.

Then something was wrong, the trance lifting. Its sturdy balance of force, resistance, release had shifted and the rhythm came apart for me, undone by an unfocused fear that I had forgotten something important, left it behind, and now would be lost.

The wind had quit. Down the line, cutting slowed, then stopped as each of us surfaced into the perfect calm. Left alone by the wind, the fire frittered, but came perceptibly now down the slope, its perimeter extending in thrusts and bulges. The slope was veined with small draws, and as the flames intersected these they sluiced up them, turning the chutes into flumes of fire.

In the growing light, Cable looked reflective, as though he were trying to remember something. He must have been lining up odds: Dalton—the legend and us—against what remained to be done, against the pathology of all those fires, against this one. We could go out easily now down the line. Or we could go on. If the Santa Ana came up, the fire would heel over again and there would be plenty of time. Without the wind, we still might tie the line in before the fire reached the canyon bottom, perhaps in time to go out our line backfiring. With luck, we could turn the fire here, maybe finish it. If the fire crossed the canyon, all bets were off. We would have minutes, then, to bail off the back side of the ridge, wading down through the brush before the fire crested the ridgeline. Even the cat line wouldn't hold against a run on this slope.

Cable called for our two-minute drill. Mundeen had given it the name—a fourth-quarter drive against the clock. We would slit a scratch line to the top, the chancy minimum; then back down the line, unraveling fire behind us as we came.

We turned again to the brush, urgency and control beveling to the edge we had to have. The ridge was flushed with light, and we began to pick up radiant heat from across the canyon. The fire pulse plunged through the arteries of brush and we could feel its swell beat against us. Quirky winds veered across the steady suck of oxygen into the flames, the fire making its own weather now. I worked with absolute focus, as though mistossing one piece of brush might make the difference. But gradually, at first against my will, some part of me drew away, enlarging until at last it seemed to take in the whole hulk of the Santa Sangres, the vast, impassive brushfields, the furnace stoking itself; beneath and beyond, the night going on and on. And fourteen mortal men, flickers of flesh: negligible, there, remarkable beyond all accounting.

Then the firefront was into the canyon bottom. Too soon. And the Santa Ana was back, not full force, but with strength to deflect the head perhaps enough. And Cable hesitated, squinting into the canyon. No way of backfiring now, only the chance that without the momentum of a straight run up the ridge, the fire might not breach the line. If the line was all there. And we were so close now, so deep into this line, this season. More variables, the wrong certainties piling up, the whole configuration tilting, but the equation still possible. And Cable turned his back on the pouring light. And we went on.

And from this turning I remember a whole, simultaneous—sequence only because the mind insists on continuity, divided from time by the heat which came first in surges and then with the steady, molten force of an open forge. Smoke boiled across the line, eddied, and came again leaving us staggered and stung. Jimmy into a high, keen singing. No compression, no finesse, cutting from passion fused with panic. Desperate with exhaustion, choking for air in a fragment of clearing; a sound, a dry staccato clicking and a jag of terror through me above my level fear of the flames. Cable, Jimmy, Speyer, me: in a charmed circle of clear air we pivoted towards the buzzing. A diamondback, driven by the fire, lay coiled near Jimmy, tongue flickering, neck tensed back. Jimmy, leaning, cocking his hook, belt hanging free, buckle gone. Swinging as the snake struck, splitting gristle and bone. Rigid as the fangs went in above his boot. And held. Slowly, turning, his hook in a great circle above his head hurled at Speyer; then off the ridge, lunging down, screeching, into the fire. Speyer on one knee, missed. A crouch beyond reflex. The slope of fire, waves of flame surging and cresting its surface. Cable speaking into the radio, a deep stain down the arm of his fire shirt, saying we were taking casualties, saying we needed the helitack medical team when they could get off the ground, saying we were seven chains short and it didn't look like we'd be able to tie the line in. I stood, dead center, pierced by the end of Jimmy's wail, a silence into which no words could ever be spoken. Cable's hands on me, steady, but moving me back and forth: the hook, the hook clattered into some rock behind the line, find it, never leave a weapon, we might still, it might get us out. And away from me into the smoke where others had clustered. Mechanically, stiff-legged to keep them from buckling, through the brush: a bare patch of scaly shale, the rigid sparwork of dead brush, the hook. Turning back; not going back, I think, only turning. There. Down the line, rising out of the firestorm, a fire whirl: malignant, swollen beyond itself, beyond natural law, into a fire spout funneling up hundreds of feet. Tilting, coming up the ridge, a pulse of white flame at its center, riding the edge of the fire; lateral sheets of flame drawn to its base, shreds of burning brush hurled far across the line. Spot fires coming up behind me, the back side of the ridge breaking out. Speyer. In a thinning of smoke, at the end of our line, as far as we had come. Fading and coming back in the smoke-clotted light—a darkening, a density, the mouth of a tunnel in the mountain of smoke. And the fire spout, spasming free, a convulsion of flame bending to him. Who did not run but waited, faced into it, not burning yet but as a man lit by his bones, luminous. Bulky smoke took me down, blinded. On the ground I could breathe a little. Scuffing around on my knees, keeping my back to it as the worst heat came from one way and another, I sloshed my canteens over my shirt and jeans, the last of it on my bandana. Someone screaming "no no no no no no no." A voice so gone in terror and pain it seemed unshaped by a human mouth. Yanked my shirt up where my neck was blistering. The orange rolled out, down my thigh. A little clown. Heat steamed my lungs as I gagged for air. Tearing at the orangehide till it came apart. A chunk stuffed in my mouth, my nose jammed in the rest. Whining against the pain in my hands. The bandana, knotted, finally, across my face. In a huddle against the earth, rigid, jerking. The fire roar closed.

In the ashen light before full dawn, I slanted in and out of consciousness. My body jolted with pain; my mind, treasonous, saying "let go, let go." Lucid, I thought to crawl to the line, to the others, to be found when the rescue team came up. To move an arm blinded me with fibers of light; moving more, I passed out. I tried for the hook, to prop it up, to tie my scorched bandana to it as a sign. My mind eddied away in pain; coming back, I could not remember what I had been trying to do. I lay still then, listening to the rasp of my breath. As I seeped towards death, in focus beyond my filmy sight was the panorama of earth and sky I had inhabited earlier in the night. My last act on the ridge was to resist that sanctuary; my last awareness, if I left my body for it, this time I would not be back.

Blowtorched, brush burns quickly. By dawn, the search and rescue team had managed to get up the ridge. They found most of the crew on the line. Cavenaugh died before anything could be done for him. Moya lasted long enough for the morphine to ease his way out. They found Stinson alive under Cable's body. Gridding the area, they found more bodies, then me. Weaving through my delirium, I remember the face of a black man on the team, remember wondering if my eyes had been scorched. And trying to explain why I wasn't on the line, that I hadn't been running away. And a refrain, softly, from someone I couldn't see, as they worked on me: "Oh shit, oh shit, oh shit."

The National Guard managed to get a big Chinook in on the ridge. Stinson died in the air. The hospital, prepared for fourteen men, got one.

It took them several hours to locate Jimmy. Speyer's body was never found.

The lead men of a regional investigation team got there in the afternoon. They took photographs and marked the locations of bodies. The wind was still too high to risk bringing in another helicopter. Dalton went back down the ridge by hand, one by one, the rubber body bags making small squishing sounds as they swayed and faintly ticking as the wind buckshot them with grit.

My burns were serious, but once they got an IV started on the ridge and brought me out of shock, they didn't think they'd lose me. I had second-degree burns over my butt and the backs of my thighs and calves; third-degree on one wrist along a gap between my leather glove and the cuff of my fire shirt, on one ear and the side of my neck, and in a semicircle around my waist where the elastic of my shorts had melted and stuck to the skin. My lungs had been singed slightly, and they pumped me with antibiotics that checked the pneumonia that developed. There was an early skin graft on my neck; a touch-up graft later, and some reconstructive work on my ear. Everything healed. Even the pain was routine. I was off the critical list in four days, out of the hospital in three weeks.

The doctor who flew in on the Chinook—and, later, the Forest Service investigation team—pieced it together for me. Apparently, the area where Jimmy's hook landed had been burned over in a spot lightning fire earlier in the season. It gave me a margin of forty feet or so where there was nothing for the fire but me. The fire shirt and hard hat, my wet jeans and bandana, and staying down gave me maximum protection. But it was the orange, the doctor said, that probably saved my life. Breathing through its pulp must have filtered the worst of the heat. Without it, he said, my lungs would have been seared; I would have suffocated. He wanted to know how I came to use the orange that way. I had no answer.

A week after I left the hospital, I flew back to the ridge with the investigation team. The sky was a stunning blue, the air so vivid it was as though we flew through a dome of crystal. Coming in, I could see Dalton's line branding the ridge, the small distance between the line's end and the rockslide. From our line, ridge after ridge, the land was a sullen gray. The downwash of the helicopter billowed ash and grit as the pilot brought us in. Gaudy plastic ribbons streamed from tall metal stakes until the engine was shut down. They marked the location of bodies.

On the ground, I was able to answer more of their questions. I tried to gauge where I had last seen Speyer. The fire behavior specialist said they would make one more sweep of the area, but that a fire spout could generate temperatures beyond 3,000 degrees. Even bones, he said, were combustible in that kind of heat.

Before we flew out, I walked away from them, back to the place where I hadn't died. I waited for the right gesture to occur. Nothing happened. A blue ribbon hung from the metal post. It meant that the man found here had lived.

A Region 3 hotshot foreman came over after a bit. His name was Slocum. Years later, in Wyoming, I was his division boss on a fire.

"I just wanted you to know what the score was. I think you got a right." He stubbed his boot against the post and worked a wad of tobacco around in his cheek. "They hauled me out here to make it look square, like Cable was getting a fair shake. If they decide to pin this on Cable, I can't do nothing about it and neither can you. They found a bunch of prescriptions for pain killers in his office. It sounds like they can work it out that the pills screwed him up enough to make a difference. That way Uncle's off the hook. You were here. I've been an inch away more than once. I heard what you said, and now I've seen the ground. I'm not saying I wouldn't have done it different. And I'm not saying he couldn't have pulled it off. You can never tell. But once that fire spout cooked up, you were finished. When your luck turns like that, there's not one damn thing you can do."

FIRE SEASON

Slocum leaned and spit a glob of juice.

"There's one thing bothers me though, and I'd be lying if I didn't say so. I heard a tape of his last transmission. He sounded OK. He sounded like he was calling in for the time of day. But he was asking for artillery. He was calling for a strike on top of his position."

We lifted off the ridge and the Bell pivoted south, heading back, nose tilted down like a hound. Below, the Backbone Burn marked the Santa Sangres like the smudged print of an ancient beast—fossil evidence that something awesome had passed this way.

When it finally appeared, the team's report didn't single out Cable. There was no mention of the pain killers, nor his last radio message. They did hold him accountable for not backing off as soon as the Santa Ana started breaking down and in that, I guess, they were right.

Still, so much of it was beyond his control, beyond his knowing, even. The Santa Ana had started to break up treacherously two days before the meteorologists had predicted. The line scout had missed a stand of dead oak in the canyon bottom. The fire got into their crowns and bridged across to our ridge far faster than would have happened in pure brush. And the fire spout: that burning at the margin of the natural world, like a judgment out of the Old Testament. It closed the circle on Dalton, cutting off the back side of the ridge as our way out.

The investigation team got these contingencies into the report. They managed to suggest that much of what happened was a result of what might once have been called acts of God. They conveyed this, of course, in passive voice and nonattributive syntax, with jargoned vocabulary like a radioactive mutant of ordinary language. God himself was never actually mentioned.

In the end, then, there was no blame, or blame spread so thinly it rippled the placid surface of the Forest Service only for those attuned to bureaucratic nuance.

So I outlived that fire season, then outgrew it in many ways.

But it laid down a core that set the shape the rings of succeeding years would take. I finished up at Humboldt State and signed on permanently with the Forest Service. I thought I'd see more country, in more ways, in the Forest Service; could, perhaps, stand a little on the side of the land against the coming of numbers. It has turned out that way, more or less. Even fire held nothing for me I couldn't stare down or sweat out.

Still, there are two ghosts of memory, sometimes almost palpable, that have accompanied me. Speyer and Jimmy feel as alive to me now as they ever were. Perhaps it is because they had a dimension, an amplitude that kept them beyond the decay of time.

They are with me tonight, as mist sifts over the ridges and the rain spreads like a benediction. I have probed again and again, no doubt altering their shape in memory. I have been as careful as I know how, but there is no one to check this against. I am my only source, my own story, my solitary auditor. They are in my hands, as I am in theirs. Linked like binary stars, Speyer and Jimmy circle each other, their center of gravity beyond surmise, their acts in the mortal world tangible as ball lightning, as luck or love. And as inexplicable.

Tonight, at Oscar's desk, rubbing the old itch of my wrist scar, I look out into the rain I cannot see, think of the warm weight of my wife as she curls in bed, listening through sleep for the sound of my truck in the drive. Beneath the rain, the Santa Sangres swarm with the coming of a new season; behind the rain, the world curves away beyond my season of vision.

Figuring the Quiet

I had pretty much a quiet life those years. Mostly it was that way except for one thing which could have happened anytime so it doesn't count for much in figuring the quiet. My stand used to be smack in the middle of the ripest fruit country you'd ever like to see. The old highway which is still there in places runs alongside the Yakima River and just where the river bottoms out of the fast water is where my stand was.

That particular summer was the best money I ever made or expect to. The cots and cherries started coming in about when everybody was driving weekends to the mountains, and I had just painted my stand which was getting a little old and pocked up. I had also leased a Coca-Cola machine which was automatic and could hold forty-eight bottles. So without bragging on myself you can believe I was getting along pretty good.

Then one afternoon late which was slow on business being a Monday, I was setting out some Bings and determining on how much I should charge for plums when my attention was distracted by this little twig of a Mexican boy maybe twelve or thirteen walking down the side of the road packing a gunnysack along over his shoulder. I watched him casual and going on about my own business, as it was plain enough he only had one arm and I wasn't wanting to stare. So he kept on walking and looking nowhere but straight ahead until he was out front of my stand where he stopped. I went right on setting out the cherries and he just stood there taking me in which made me feel a little funny. Without looking I could see he was wearing some red corduroy pants and a flannel shirt that went clear down to his knees with one sleeve crossed up over the other shoulder and tied to the end of that gunnysack.

Some situations a man's got to squat on a while but for numerous reasons, some of them good and some of them jumpy, I settled my mind right off that it would be better if he wasn't standing there in that plain a sight. So I went and got two nickels from the cashbox and bought us both a Coke which I opened. I held one out at him and says I expected he wouldn't mind something to wash the dust down which was just a way of talking as the state had paved the road twelve years ago. Sometimes I'd tell that to a customer and then say sort of offhand that it didn't make much sense talking about something to wash the cement down as once it's laid down cement don't tend to come up like dust. That used to be one of my little jokes for the city people and you could tell it tickled them.

Anyhow the little guy just keeps looking, me all the time holding the bottle out with drips of water running down the grooves. Just as I am wondering if maybe I should pretend I got both bottles for myself, he starts to walk up with that gunnysack which I noticed impeded him a plain bit. He takes the Coke cautious and goes over to one side of my stand where he sits down on the ground not ever once taking his eyes off from me. He never said thank you or any such thing but I say some folks aren't talkers or maybe he didn't know any English although the young ones pick it up pretty quick. However by the way he went after that Coke you could tell he was liking it all right so I went on about my business.

When I got done I went around back with the empty crate as I like to keep the stand tidy and anyway what can a one-arm kid tied to a gunnysack steal in the time it takes me to get there and back? I sort of hurried anyway and then feel a little silly as I am out of breath from hurrying which I'm not used to and he is still sitting there except that he had poured some of the Coke into the palm of his hand and was feeding it to a kitten whose head and front legs were sticking out of his shirt pocket.

Now if you never ran a fruit stand you'd most likely want to figure out how he got that Coke in his hand with only one arm or maybe remark on a cat that drank soda pop. But if you've been in the business you'd know that cats have a way of jumping up and going to sleep where they aren't wanted and sometimes trying their claws on the crates and raking the merchandise between the slats, not to mention some other things.

So I decided that nevermind my funny feelings about the kid, things had come around so I could ask him to move along without feeling bad about it. Allowing for the fact that I invited him in however, it wouldn't have been right to ask him to leave before the Coke was all gone even if he had taken a disadvantage of my hospitality by sneaking in a cat. So acting uninterested like a doctor poking around where it wasn't hurting you till then, I sort of walk over where the early pears are. When I get to the pears I happen to take out my watch and say so he can hear me that it's getting to be about that time meaning I was going to close up and get some supper.

By now the kid and his cat have done in all the Coke and I can tell by the way the cat is licking his paws with a funny look to him that he is eyeing my crates for a place to hide or worse. Just as I have made up my mind to say scat straight out to the both of them this Buick with a black trunk strapped on the roof drives up with a man and a woman and the man gets out.

Now I'll say right off that looking through the windshield she wasn't exactly the most beautiful lady you'd ever like to set your eyes to. She was pretty enough all right but the kind of pretty reservation Indian girls have just about the time they can see they're going to get old and married and fat but can't quite believe it yet. Indian pretty we call it around here and I guess you could get the idea if you ever kept any kind of eye on a Indian summer. But when you tried to figure her next to that fellow she was driving with—well it was maybe like seeing a peach tree growing next to an electricity pole. For one thing he had a beard for which there's no reason I know of besides plain laziness. Then he was all suited up without even his coat unbuttoned nevermind the vest which even the city men have sense enough not to do in the summers around here.

So while I was pretty much staring and sizing up the two of them, this man starts to walk around the car real tippytoe so as not to raise the dust and all the time watching her like she was going to jump out and run away or something for which I wouldn't have blamed her. When he gets there he opens the door and takes her by the elbow like she was an old woman and says about her freshening up and him seeing about buying some fruit except that he said it in long skinny words that kept on going a while before they stopped. She was still just standing there so he says the same thing all over again only slower and nodding his head up and down and maybe he pinched her arm but so you couldn't see for certain.

Well right from the get you could tell he didn't know much about getting on with folks but I expect you got to look out for that from someone who goes around in a suit in the middle of summer. However if you want to make a living you can't get too touchy about your customers and I noticed he was patting his billfold to make sure it hadn't got lost. But just as soon as I decide to be tolerate I wish that I hadn't because for sure he has seen that I am and walks up so close I can smell the whiskey and wintergreen on his breath and says right in my face something about my facilities.

It didn't give me much comfort to see I had sized him up right. Except for the beard he sounded a lot like the county agent who tries to tell us all sorts of fanciness about our orchards. However after a bit he said something about rustic which I happened to understand all right and I was just about ready to ask him direct what it was he wanted when he stuck his face up even closer and said real loud was there a bathroom anywhere. He still had a hand on his billfold so I was obligated to be tolerate so I pointed my thumb to show him there was a place around behind. He didn't say anything but just turned around to the girl who was hanging back and took her to the car which was all right with me.

I just then remembered about the boy and the cat and got one of those hot flashes in my stomach at what they maybe did when I wasn't paying attention. However what he was doing when I turned around was carving with a knife on a dried-up McIntosh which he was holding between his knees and must have got from that gunnysack as it was way too early for Macs and the sack was untied from his shirtsleeve and setting right beside him on the ground. Behind my back I could hear that the Buick wasn't wanting to start which was no surprise as a man like that was just the sort who could flood an engine.

However neverminding about him I determined right then that my mind was made up. Anybody who would sneak out a knife when all parties concerned weren't looking irregardless of his age or intentions wasn't anywhere near the sort of person I wanted around the stand. So just when I had my attention fixed on moving the boy along, here's the man hollering out the window did I know anything about starting cars. Well I know some, but not being the hollering kind I didn't say so. About then my stomach starts working and there's three people not counting the cat and car standing on my fork you might say which is just what comes of giving folks too much slack. And now my attention has gotten divided again which is not helped by the man getting out and trotting over to me. He didn't trot any better than he could start a car but I figured he didn't want my advice on trotting so I didn't tell him so. He stopped hollering before he got up to me and said he could make it worth my while to start his car which I told him I couldn't do because anybody could hear that the battery had got run down while he was flooding the engine. So what he does instead is call on my telephone for a tow truck. Then he buys two Coca-Colas and gets the girl out of the car where she has been and they make themselves at home on one of my benches.

I can tell the man is sizing me up by the way he looks all around the stand but never once in my direction. When he's done he takes a sip of Coke to pretend he wasn't doing anything. Then he gets a handkerchief from his suitcoat and looks surprised when a bunch of handbills falls out on the floor. He picks them up like he's never before that minute seen them. Then he reads one over and hands it to me. His picture is on it with the girl who is dressed up to look like a Indian except with the tops of her breasts sticking out. The writing said he was a doctor and a professor and that the girl couldn't talk but could tell what was in people's pockets and things like that without looking. The handbill said she did it all by vibrations and then she vibrated to the professor who told you what she meant. When I gave it back to him, the girl who had been sitting there so you wouldn't notice just like that grabbed for the handbill but she wasn't very fast and he got it back in his pocket.

It was hard to figure what she'd want with it as it was a pretty fuzzy picture and didn't look a lot like her. I didn't say so but I was interested which the professor must have saw because he said she had funny ideas about her picture and he had to be careful because one time she stole all the handbills and got clear to Boise before he caught up to her. He was looking mad about remembering that and like he might smack her so I tried to look like I might smack him if he did so instead he asked me if I'd like a demonstration at one-half price which was ten cents. I told him I already knew what was in my pocket. You can bet he wasn't ready for that but he acted like he wasn't surprised and went right ahead and asked the boy if he wanted one for a nickel. The boy just keeps cutting at the apple so the doctor picks up his Coke and keeps drinking it.

I have given up by now seeing that everything I've tried has not budged one of them and to tell the truth I am interested in people of all kinds. And anyhow a shiny Buick out front isn't going to hurt business even if there isn't any. So I get out my broom and start to sweep around just to look busy and like I would be there whether they are or not. However I started to notice that now and then the boy is eyeing the girl and the professor is eyeing the boy steady, and sure as cherry pits I get a sudden feeling in my stomach which don't mean I'm hungry.

So when the boy puts away his knife and the kitten and ties on his sack and walks slow with the apple over to the girl my sap is running and I'm glad I've got hold of my broom although it is not a baseball bat which I wished it was. When he holds out the apple I am close enough to see that it looks exactly like her face except for the color which is not the same. She grabs for it and the professor does too but the boy is pretty fast for just one arm. He holds it back a ways so she can still see it real clear and then he shimmies it in his bag and starts to go out to the road.

What happens then changes my mind about the broom which I stop sweeping with but cemetery sure don't pick up off the floor and try not to look like I might have. The girl has got up and the professor grabs ahold of her arm and then the boy is turned around with that knife in his hand which he throws. Nobody is screaming which I am thankful for but the girl is walking over to the boy and the professor is not moving one inch because the knife is stuck in a crate right by his shoulder and the boy has another knife in his hand which is a lot meaner than the first one. Then the boy walks over like a stalking cat and gets his knife back. When the two of them are gone so you can't see them, the professor starts to shake and keeps on shaking but so you couldn't tell if he was mad or scared or both. He didn't take half a step after them. I think about it for a while and decide I am not much sorry for the professor. When the tow truck gets here at dark the professor climbs in and goes off and I sell a pint of Bings to Mel Stonecrofter's oldest boy who is driving.

I expect all that was about early July. So I had put it out of my mind absolutely by September when I closed up one weekend and went up to the Wenatchee County Fair. I don't get surprised by much but what I saw at that fair came pretty close to it.

What happened was I saw the one-arm boy and the girl again. It was just green luck that I did as the crowd was pretty thick around their booth. So I keep one hand on my billfold and sort of hang around the back of the crowd for a while. I notice the girl is wearing high-heeled shoes and a red swimming suit. She is standing on a little platform with her back and arms up flat against a board and her legs spread apart. The boy is throwing knives which doesn't seem to worry her as he's pretty good and can stick most of them so close you couldn't get goose grease between them and her. The kitten is more rightly a cat now and rubs around some on her ankles while she is up there. When all the knives are stuck in she sits down on one of those metal folding chairs and eats some Cracker Jack and an ice cup which is mostly melted. She never stops watching the boy however who gets out his old sack which I remember and sets a bunch of pieces of wood on the counter. A man who buys one shoves past me and nevermind the shove I can see he's carved the wood to look like the top part of the girl except without her swimming suit. The bottom part looks like legs except that they're hinged on and the man works them a couple of times like a nutcracker.

So I looked over the rest of the fair and purchased a nice doll for my niece and went home. After that I never came across neither one of them again however much I was on the lookout at fairs and the like. I truly think on the two of them sometimes but I can't tell you any more because that's all I know.

Baja

Warm again. Peter swallowed with a flinch and set the bottle down. Mexican dishwater beer. The cafe's butane refrigerator worked intermittently. When it did, the beer and everything else was usually frozen. No one but Peter seemed to care very much, or even notice. If he never left the cafe, he would know all he ever needed to about the country.

He lit a cigarette and thumbed the match at a bad-smelling dog asleep on the floor of the cafe veranda. The wooden match made a small clatter on the concrete. They had chosen Puertocitos because friends had said that on the gulf side of Baja one could still find Mexican beach towns that did not pander to tourists for a living. Here, there were some ranches in the hills, a bedraggled fishing fleet, a small bauxite mine, few Americans. Peter drew his thumb along the abrasive side of the matchbox, then opened it and struck another match.

"Peter?" The woman, angular and very pretty, sat at the table with him.

Peter turned to her, but his eyes still held the match, watching it char and bend above the flame. When the heat reached his fingers, he shook the match. It kept burning. He shook it again, sharply, and dropped it to the floor.

"Peter, don't be like this. Please?" The woman reached out, resting her fingers on his wrist. The dark gold curve of her wedding band seemed almost to merge with her tan. Peter pulled away and reached for the beer.

"All right." She stood and began to unbutton the blouse which covered her bathing suit.

Peter watched the blouse fall open without seeming to. Two weeks of sun and salt water. Full and shining from it, the ends of her dark blonde hair turning white, she had become what travel posters promise. But in three months, maybe less? Looking away across the coastal scrublands, Peter tightened his face against expression. Yes, when she was five months pregnant, drooping and clumsy . . . The image rose up and he let the words swell like a fragrance, dissolving into the air of that vision. He crossed his legs slowly, still ready to wince at the sunburn that had stopped hurting days ago. He had not been in the water since. Sarah, pale as he when they came, took the sun easily. She had even spent two blinding afternoons on the bay with the fishermen.

His wife finished folding her blouse and laid it on the table. Perfect. Folded easily, casually, without wrinkles. Peter frowned.

"Don't go out too far. One of the boys saw mullet jumping off the point this morning."

Sarah watched his face for inflection, and Peter began to move the bottle slowly between his palms. Across the arc of bay, sun glazed the water. He would win this time, either way he would win. If she said "Sharks?" he could shrug and she would know the accusation. A wife who understood that mullet jumping meant sharks in the water needed no guardianship, no husband. Her alternative was to ask why mullet had anything to do with being careful. This would be a larger if more complicated victory, for he had heard a fisherman explaining this to her their first day in the village. She knew. If she chose to pretend she did not, he would make it clear, lethally clear, that he had caught her again in the deception of trying to need him.

"I won't go in if you want."

Bitch! Peter increased the pressure of his hands on the bottle and shrugged. Sarah tilted her head; then reached over, plucked the beer from his hands, and, running across the veranda and slender rim of sand, splashed out into the water, bottle held high above her head.

"Come and get it!" A swollen wave broke behind her and she was surrounded by foam.

Peter got up and went inside. The cafe had three tables where fishermen, barefoot, drank beer and waited for the afternoon calm. The stools along the bar were empty. Peter chose one farthest from the tables.

"Carlos, *una cerveza.*"

The owner put down his newspaper and got a beer from the refrigerator. He set it in front of Peter. Peter touched the bottle, then shoved it back across the counter.

"*Demasiado calor.*" For a month before they came, he had studied his old Spanish text at work. He brought with him a pocket dictionary he kept hidden in his shaving kit. Carlos, the only person he had any reason to talk to, spoke English to Peter.

"Ah, yes. It is very hot today." Carlos took a sip from the bottle and handed it back.

"I don't mean the weather." Peter gestured at the bottle. "Your beer tastes like hot piss."

"Yes, the beer is warm also." Carlos nodded several times and went back to his paper.

A muted run of Spanish passed among the tables. Peter clenched inside and set his teeth. Pukeheads! He tightened around the word. Talk and drink and fish and screw and die. Your sons will die in Tijuana, and they will speak English. It passed, and Peter sipped his beer, carefully wiping the foam from his mouth with the back of his hand.

And my child? He smelled the ocean and skidded helplessly back. The night Sarah had put his hand on her stomach and kissed him, they had gone out to dinner and had drunk too much wine and had been very happy. The fact of his child inside her had pleased Peter in a way he could only partly explain. It had somehow promised completion: connection with a real and separate world he had spent his life imitating— posturing, miming, all the while fearful of being found out. But now Mrs. Peter Madison was going to have his child—his. This fact had grown in him like moist new life. A fastening, yes, the child would be the filament to splice his life to that bond which passed among other men.

But then this promise had scalded away in a sudden recognition. She had tried to cheat him again; to do for him what she thought he could not do for himself. His participation in the child became a function of her manipulation, became incidental and binding. He took another swallow of beer and was surprised that it was gone.

"*Una más*, Carlos."

He was bound, clever bitch, to the child. To show her that he knew, to name the child the device that it was, would be to condemn it. And in condemning his child, he would pass judgment on himself. Formal, final judgment.

Carlos set the beer down. The fishermen were no longer talking. Peter looked at them. Several were drinking, two seemed asleep, three were playing cards. Although the game had just started, the young man at the table already had most of the money. Peter turned away and looked at his watch. It had stopped. In front of him, the clock above the bar kept time without an hour hand. It seemed close to noon and Peter thought about ordering something to eat. Instead, he finished his beer and went outside to the toilets. He didn't hear the voices until he had latched the door.

"It's mine. Give it here, Vicente." The petulant whine of a child, complaining more from habit than conviction. Peter listened.

"No . . . " drawn out, variegated, Mexican. "I say that all right you have it yesterday. Now I will take it back."

The words, a statement of fact, contained no argument.

"Come on, Vicente, I'll let you use my pole."

"No, Billy. I catch better my way. My father tells that people need poles because only that they do not know how to come to the fish." Again the tone in which he might have said the bad storms come out of the south and the wind blows down from the hills at night.

Peter held back a cough. He could not remember Billy, though he must have belonged to one of the summer American families around the point. Nor had he any notion of what was at stake. But he knew, knew in a quick motion of pain, that

Vicente was right and Billy wrong. The plea embedded in Billy's whine reached him, the distorted echo of a familiar voice. It was a plea, not for justice, but license.

"Gimme it!" A body thumped into the boards of the latrine.

"No, Billy. I don't fight with you. Get up now and go home."

"You bastard! Chicken bastard!"

Peter leaned and looked out through a chink in the planking. Billy was on his feet, shouting. Vicente was walking away. Billy scooped up a rock and flung it after him. It missed. Vicente kept walking.

"Your mother screws!"

Vicente stopped and jerked around.

"You say what my mother?"

"She screws, she fucks—shit, prick, cock!"

Vicente dropped the turtle he carried and came after Billy. Billy ran.

Peter urinated, then unhooked the door and stepped out. The wind had fallen, and in the west a field of thunderheads had begun to rise above the Sierras. The fishermen had come out of the cantina and were moving along the beach to their boats. They waved to Sarah's shouts from the surf. Peter went inside and sat again at the bar.

When Sarah came from the water, she found five empty bottles lined in a careful row on the bar. Their labels lay in ragged piles beside them. She went away without speaking. Later Peter asked Carlos if it ever rained. Carlos thought about it, rubbing the back of his neck with the palm of his hand.

"No. We have the sea."

Peter said he wanted to know if it rained. Carlos shrugged and took the empty bottles away.

By evening Peter was drunk. He and Sarah were on the veranda with the fishermen, who sat together at a large table, each sipping a beer in the late light. Peter watched the small breasts of the girl who served their meal. The girl worked with distant efficiency, sparrowing quick looks at Sarah.

When the table was cleared, Sarah asked if he would like to walk on the beach. Peter shrugged and pushed back his chair.

"Go ahead if you like." The words were spoken slowly, shaped by the tongue with care.

"Please don't drink any more."

He shrugged again and watched Carlos come up from the beach and onto the veranda, carrying two buckets of seawater. He raised each slightly and nodded.

"For the crab we catch tomorrow."

"*Quiero un cerveza.*" Peter was looking past him to the sea.

"Ah . . . " Carlos eased the buckets to the concrete. "But there is no more before tomorrow if the truck comes."

Peter kept looking at the water.

"Get me some beer you puking spic," he said in separate, measured words.

"Yes, *es lástima*, there is no more." Carlos picked up the pails. Peter shrugged off Sarah's arm and stood. His chair fell to the concrete, a turtle spun on its back in the sun far from water. The fishermen watched across their beer.

"It's going to get a hell of a lot more *lástima* if I don't get some beer right now. I've spent enough money in this slum—"

"Oh Carlos, I'm sorry." Sarah took Peter's arm again and he stumbled against the table shaking it off.

"Damn it! Leave me alone!"

Sarah looked from Peter to Carlos, then to the fishermen.

"Ramón? Please?" A young Mexican got up and moved cautiously across the veranda. Peter spun around to face him as he came. It was the one who had been winning at cards. The one he had been expecting all his life.

"Get your stinking brown greasy body back where it belongs." The words were swollen now, thick and fumbling across each other.

Ramón angled his head. "Señor, you have the most beautiful woman. You want to drink and be angry still." And more softly, in profound bewilderment: "You are a fool, señor."

Peter swung at him, missing as Ramón stepped back. Peter caught his balance, started to swing again, then stopped. He lowered his arms, stood still, then took his matchbox from the table. In the sudden vacuum, the match erupted in a sulfurous flare. Peter smiled viciously and bowed, slowly, formally, to Ramón.

"I light a small candle for your mother who fucks donkeys."

Then he was crying, crying even before Ramón's fist drove into his stomach and he crumpled, the matches clattering across the concrete. Crying from a grief so arid the salt of the blood in his mouth fell like rain upon that withering sorrow.

Long Green

On Friday nights I pick up the sitter, a tight little piece who thinks I look like Jack Nicholson, drop off Marlene and whatever friend she's talking to this week at the movies, and take it easy in the Chev out to Mel's. I used to wind out the last block of State and take the little hump in the bridge at sixty-five, but the Chev needs new shocks and besides I can't afford any tickets right now.

At Mel's I do a quick count of how many Fords and Chevys there are in the lot, including trucks. It's a little habit I got into and keep up even though it doesn't exactly mean anything. If there was more Fords, I used to figure I was in for a good night. A man drives a Ford, you know his hands are going to be so greasy and banged up from working on it all the time he can't have much feel for a cue. These days, though, even Chevys fall apart.

Walking up to the side door, I always have to think about which way it opens. It's funny how little things like that get away from you. When I get inside I say hello around, grab Karen, who pretends she doesn't like it, and put my quarter on the table. Eight years ago, when I was back from the Army, I liked to watch how the regulars looked at each other when my quarter went down. But I don't pay attention to that kind of stuff anymore.

I generally have a couple of beers before I shoot, to sort of loosen up and give me a chance to check out the competition. The place is OK, but it hasn't been itself since Ron bought out Mel a couple of years back. The really good sticks don't come here now because Ron won't let you play for more than five, but some of the kids shoot an interesting game. When my quarter starts coming up, I notice lately how I get sticky—not in the palms, but between my fingers. I was talking to Phil the other day at the union hall and he said I should see a doctor because his sister-in-law sweated like that when she started dying of cancer.

But I use plenty of talc and that smooths the action out. Anyway it's the stick that's important. I got to get one of my own pretty soon; nothing fancy, just something I can count on. The company's supposed to be making some deal with the Japs that would crank up the line again. Phil said we're sure to get called back; maybe even suck up some of that sweet overtime. When we do, I figure I owe myself something.

Anyhow, Ron won't throw out a cue till it's busted, and he gets away with it because the kids don't even bother to check for warp or a bad tip. Most of them put so much juice on the ball it doesn't matter anyway. I've got to admit they're lucky, though. Luck will beat experience without luck oftener than you'd think, and I've been in kind of a slump lately.

I think it started when I blew a couple of five-dollar games to some jerk that didn't know which end to spot the balls on. After that I guess I started pressing. I took too long lining up shots, talked too much when I missed, and started thinking about the long green every time I had to go all the way down the table to pick up a ball. I use to be a sweet position player. I could make a razor cut and still set up just about anywhere on the table I wanted. But lately the ball isn't alive coming off the tip and the corner pockets feel like bumpers instead of funnels. I used to be surprised when I missed.

There are a couple of things that bother me most, though. One is that the regulars don't like to shoot me. It isn't that I don't pay up and there's nothing funny about me but they just don't. Maybe they think I'll rub off on them or something. For a while there they rode me when my game was off. Now they sort of act almost like they hope I'll beat them. I don't know, but all it'll take is one good night and they'll be making up lies to explain where their folding money went. Right now I mostly get games with guys who only hang around a couple nights.

But the other thing is worse. It is really bad. Back just recently I used to wind up for the fast kids with the hot sticks. I'd let them cock around the table for a while and then . . . it was sweet. Now when I come up against one I get a sick little rush like I just twisted my ankle, and the kids fool around—try double banks, play the jukebox, hustle tit. Nobody watches me shoot anymore.

I know I haven't lost the touch; once you got the touch you can't ever really lose it unless you get blind or crippled up or old or something. I never was much for banks, but I can still cut with anybody. It's the straight-in shots that give me trouble. Maybe it's confidence, I don't know. It used to be all one thing, all together—the smoke, the game, the music, everything. Now there's me, the stick, the pocket, and two balls. And it doesn't fit together anymore.

Ron wishes I'd drink somewhere else but he's too cheap to say so. He's afraid I'll get tired of losing and start some trouble. If I wanted to I could tell him he don't have to worry. Pool is different than being laid off. Pool takes nerve and talent, and getting stuff out of the way so you can get back in the game is just as close as the next rack.

I read lately where Cale Yarborough won the Firecracker Four Hundred, and he said the trick was to just step in there and do what you knew you could do. I thought maybe I'd call him up about that, but Marlene used the sports page to wipe up where the dog pissed and anyway I don't think it said where he was going next.

On Tour with Max

We're heading west, somewhere near the Texas/New Mexico line, driving from Canyon to Socorro. Max is in the back seat drinking Shiner Beer and hiccuping. He has been complaining about his rough handling in the question-and-answer session after last night's reading. The girl didn't look like the sort who would mix it up in public, although you really can't tell anymore, but she knew Max's early poetry a lot better than he did and was grimly partisan about its bald misogyny. When Max tried to jolly her out of a scrap, she creamed him, and the local faculty host had to step in flapping it all away and inviting everybody to the reception. Max drank and sulked his way through the party, but I got him back to the motel before any serious damage was done.

We're on our way to New Mexico Tech because Max's last live-in was a grant writer and twenty-five years ago Maximilian Pfluger was a big item in American poetry. John Ciardi called him a "pivotal countermotion in American letters." Max's friend parlayed this history into a National Endowment grant for a reading tour. Why I'm here is that the grant has a gimmick designed to give a younger poet some exposure while the colleges take an old gray reputation to the bank. Happily for Max, most faculty members apparently don't read once they leave graduate school, so reputations on the circuit lag a generation or so.

Unofficially, I'm expected to keep Max mostly in line: colorful, but on time for the next reading. Before I signed on, an NEA staffer sized me up over lunch, pointing out that NEA didn't need any bad press in this political climate and that the organization would certainly want to review my own grant needs following a successful tour.

As it turns out, keeping Max in line hasn't really been much of a chore. He is generally no worse than cranky, and when he drinks too much he tends to get sullen or sleepy instead of outrageously memorable. Still, I've had to behave more responsibly than suits me.

So instead of a one-trick pony, we give the schools a dog and pony show. Most nights, though, Max is the dog. Max fancies himself a good reader, but he is mainly loud. His gestures are all choreographed and his inter-poem patter was scripted about 1958 and hasn't changed since as far as I can tell. He still makes jokes about the Beats. There are probably literary antecedents for our act, but I don't really think I want to inquire too closely.

Although I'm the warm-up act, I usually draw a better reception. Max doesn't mind. He's getting some attention for a change, the booze is mostly free, and he's even finagled a couple of coeds into the sack. He also wets a line at every school for a visiting writer job. Some of these places are odd enough that he just might land one.

The tour is supposed to last four months and take in Texas, Oklahoma, New Mexico, Utah, Colorado, Wyoming, and Nevada. There must be two hundred schools in Texas alone, counting junior colleges, and it feels like we've hit most of them. The National Endowment deal doesn't require matching funds, so even places who've never seen a live poet order us up like examination copies of a textbook they have no intention of ever using.

Max also bootlegs a few extra readings on the side to supplement the NEA money. Mostly, though, he doesn't have the stamina to be much of a hustler so he settles for what's at hand, which is me. NEA wires us each a check every two weeks and Max is already into me for $800 I'll never see again. This is more or less OK because Max claims to have assurances that he is next in line to judge the Walt Whitman competition, although he has the decency not to remind me of this as he consummates another loan. He may be lying, but I can't take the chance that he isn't. A WW would jump-start my career, which keeps refusing to turn over, starter grinding away while my battery goes on losing juice.

Max is done with the Shiner and on into a bottle of Wild

Turkey that he lifted from the reception. I've tried to broaden his range of chemicals but he is unreconstructible: "Whatever killed Berryman and Thomas is good enough for me."

It's only April, but already the road feels like a strip of bacon under the sun and I know how much I wouldn't want to be here when summer really gets down to business. And I think about all those schools. Make no mistake: this is the satellite circuit, not the main tour. We do not stop at Southern Method-ist or Boulder or the universities of Texas or Oklahoma. We read at colleges where the faculty mournfully says, "This isn't the end of the world, but you can see it from here." Places nobody but William Stafford goes.

At most of these schools, there's an MFA from somewhere sunk up to his axles in freshman essays. They press sheaves of poems on me, asking if I'll intercede with Max on their behalf. Nobody seems to get an MFA in fiction writing anymore.

I don't tell them that Max pretends to read only the work of attractive women and that he has trouble getting his own stuff published these days. All the old editors are dropping off; the only automatic Max has left is *The Norton Anthology*, which is not a bad gimme at that. He stays in year after year because he's got something on one of the editors from graduate school days—some irregularity with sources in his dissertation, as far as I can gather.

Mostly, though, Max is out of touch in the poetry biz: he thinks Galway Kinnell is still a comer. So I read their poems. They're usually pretty competent and they all sound alike, as though they were written by sleepwalkers with elaborate sen-sibilities. They remind me of my own poems; we're all slicing up the same pie. Which is why each first book must be hailed as the appearance of a distinctive new voice. These are the manuscripts that Yale and Wesleyan and Pittsburgh will not be publishing. After a while, the poets will give up or publish at some dinky press with the half-life of a subatomic particle and be tenured or not be tenured. Some of them already divine this and are a little brittle with visiting writers and their prefer-ments.

Everywhere, though, you see them being buffed by thou-sands of freshman papers, worn smooth by the handling of chairmen and deans until there are no rough spots for a poem to stick to. At a party, a drunk and funny MFA from Cal Irvine—a lopsided man who had just switched from the raw, Third World witness poem to the somnambular lyric in hopes of publishing in *College English*, the benchmark of contemporary verse for his chairman—told me that he often thought of his senior colleagues as occupying the rocking chairs of literature while he and his like held the folding chairs of literature. There are a lot of decent, desperate people dying out there in the polar reaches of academe.

This is too depressing to dwell on, so I try as I can to make little notches in the academic conveyor belt. I tell one chair-man that the best journals are now publishing so much haiku that the Academy of American Poets has lobbied for Congress to put import quotas on Japanese verse just as it did on Toyotas. At another school, I lament to the student paper our shocking neglect of muscularity in American poetry and reveal my plans for a publishing venture to redress that disregard: The Bench Press. At a college in eastern Colorado, I whittle a bit on a dean who read three Edna St. Vincent Millay poems by way of intro-ducing me on a night when Max's aesthetic digestion gave out and I had to solo. The next morning before we left, I bought mauve ink and rose paper at the college bookstore and in my best imitation of a woman's hand wrote, "Flee, all is discov-ered." I tucked the flap into the envelope without sealing it and put it in campus mail for the dean. And so on. Nothing really outrageous, just little nicks here and there, a gesture.

The Wild Turkey has made Max nostalgic. He remembers fondly his role in making American poetry safe from Eliot. He has chronicled these campaigns before, but it comes out dif-ferent every time he repeats himself.

"We were just routing the last of the footnoters at Princeton when Bill Empson turned up on a panel and had me hanging on at the bell. But Doc Williams was working my corner that night as cut man; he patched me up and I got back after it in the next round. Even *Partisan Review* gave me the decision."

From the poetry wars of the fifties, Max moves on to literary slugfests in other venues. Though he now sags considerably, Max once fancied himself a brawler. Edmund Wilson wrote in his memoirs that Max had the sneakiest left hook in American letters. Max's history in the ring is checkered, to be sure, but he's enjoyed some notable successes. He KO'd Delmore Schwartz twice, threw James Dickey into a briar patch in Tuscaloosa, and it took Mailer a combination followed by a shove to put Max down. He also decked Dylan Thomas unfairly when Max was young and Thomas was drunk. Later, though, he loaned Thomas money. Now Max laments that nobody cares enough about poetry to get into fights about it anymore.

Max rouses himself from the legendary past to ask where we're heading. He is apprehensive to learn we have entered New Mexico. One of his former wives may be living in Santa Fe and there's apparently a matter of delinquent alimony. He worries that she might conspire to seize his earnings the way the IRS used to grab Sonny Liston's purse after every bout.

But mostly he's sorry to be leaving Texas and its petrodollars behind. Don't believe those twangy howls about the price of oil. The colleges are still awash in it like academic sheikdoms. The faculty looks as scruffy as anywhere else, but the schools are outfitting themselves handsomely. They move up a notch in NCAA football classification, they endow a chair in petroleum engineering or laissez-faire, and they amass a phalanx of new vice-presidents. They also throw elaborate receptions for itinerant poets. Max has fattened on Texas.

I figure it's going to be early evening before we make Socorro. Max's bladder is not what it used to be and we have to stop every fifty miles or so. Max has a quaint sort of modesty and always squeezes through the fence to find some kind of scrub cover. I'm not entirely sure how I feel about Max, but when I see him there hunched forward pissing into the wind and distance of New Mexico, I feel a tenderness towards him that takes me by surprise.

But sentimentality is a quick ride and we're not down the road too far before I'm filling time by erecting headlines for the tour: "Pfluger Flops in Fort Collins: Max No Factor on Poetry Scene"; "Poet Pukes at Podium: Grody to the Max." Headlines don't have much staying power either so I start doodling with dialogue. I've been thinking about trying my hand at fiction after the tour. A guy I knew in grad school is a junior editor at Simon & Schuster, which ought to give me a leg up. Anyway, it's fun to fool around with stuff I'll never get into my poetry. Usually, it goes something like this.

"When Meryl Streep takes off her clothes it's art. When I take off mine, it's $300 or 30 days."

"Your tits are prurient. Hers look like two big bowls of Wheaties or something. Besides, you didn't go to Yale."

"How do you know where she went to school?"

"I saw it in *Parade Magazine.*"

"You said you didn't read anymore."

I try to make up lines that have some ginger to them; if you can write snappy dialogue, there's no telling how far you can go.

Pretty soon it's late afternoon and the sun is going down like a slug of hot lead. We're still a hundred miles or so from Socorro and I'm getting hungry, so when we top out a long rise I'm glad to see a sign inviting us to stop at Ryan's Crossing.

Ryan's Crossing turns out to have all the comforts of home. Besides a cafe, there's a bar, general store, post office, and TV satellite receiver franchise all in roughly two and a half buildings. I gas up the Hertz while Max goes on inside. When I'm done, I park the car around the side where the pickups are. As I walk out front, I can see another truck maybe five miles out, busting its springs down a dirt road heading in, a long shroud of dust in its wake.

Max is sitting expansively at the one table that's right in the middle of things. I figure it's OK since the place is mostly empty and we'll be long gone before the Friday night crowd arrives. Max's bar etiquette is not all it should be, and he's not quite enough of a relic to get away with some of the stunts he pulls. But his luck is generally good, he's got a quick tongue in a pinch, and so far I've managed to bundle him out the door the two times when luck and wit were clearly not going to forestall mayhem.

Although the sign over the bar reads "This Property Insured by Smith & Wesson," Ryan's Crossing is pretty genial. The chili is great and the bar whiskey is cheap. There's not a video game in sight and the jukebox has some old tunes that Max plays over and over. Before I know it we're both looped and the place is full of cowboys, maybe twenty or so, all in hats they don't take off and two or three of them with women. My automatic warning light goes on, but the whiskey keeps shorting it out and I finally switch to manual override. On the one hand, no one's talked to us, which is not a good sign, but Max has no contention in him tonight and the bartender, clearly a veteran and therefore a finely tuned barometer of trouble, seems not the least uneasy.

So I'm not ready for it at all when I come out of the john and see three guys around Max at our table. The rest of the bar is quiet so I can tell right away that this is not a friendly get-together. I check the bartender, but he's going to let it happen. Max has just finished saying something, but his back is to me and I can't make it out. The cowboy across the table from him lets out a sort of laugh that seems to narrow his face.

"A poet? Well, tell you what. I never heard a real poet say a poem out loud."

"Careful, Tommy, them poets is all queers. He might take a shine to you."

"Queers and Jews."

A snappy line might still pull it out, but Max is saying nothing and the only thing I can come up with is trying to pass us off as good old goys which is not true and which I don't think anyone here would get anyway.

"So what you're going to do is climb up top that pool table and start saying poems till I tell you to quit."

"I never seed a naked poet neither. Let's strip him down, Tommy."

And I'm thinking that I should have taken up industrial hygiene in college instead of poetry. Or that with just a little luck I could have been on the road with someone a lot sweeter who stayed out of bars. Or maybe a real brawler—Jim Harrison or Philip Levine, say—people who get left alone. Instead, I've got Max who is sour and paunchy and couldn't go two rounds with a sonnet anymore. I'm still hoping that maybe we can ride it out with nothing worse than humiliation when Max swings his elbow off the table into the groin of one of the cowboys and gets knocked sideways off his chair. I figure I'm next, so I start to move and get a pool cue flat across the kidneys and then the lights go out.

When I come around, they've propped me up in a chair and Max is on the pool table. They've left Max's clothes on—a break for Max, a break for them—and he is reciting poetry. One eye is swollen and he keeps pawing at his nose, which is bleeding. He's a little unsteady, tilting above the felt, but his voice is OK and gets stronger as he goes:

The land was ours before we were the land's
She was our land more than a hundred years
Before we were her people . . .

"Hey, that ain't poetry; it's got to rhyme. You trying to mess with us?"

Max stalls and it hangs in the balance. I don't think Max knows any poems that rhyme. The man nursing his groin looks like he's getting ready to climb up on the table.

"Louise, you been to college. Is it poetry if it don't have rhymes?"

Tommy is still running things and he's going to do this right. I try to shape a prayer that whoever taught Louise her obligatory literature course did not give her a *D* and a loathing for anyone who reads poetry or writes it. I pray rather than bet, because the odds are not good.

"It used to have to rhyme. But I don't think it has to anymore."

Max coughs a couple of times and starts up again when Tommy breaks in and tells him to do it from the beginning.

When Max is through, nobody says anything until Tommy tells him to keep going. He recites two more Frosts, a Robert Penn Warren, and something I don't recognize. It turns out that once he gets rolling Max can rhyme like a bell. The next time he stops, somebody hands him a beer.

Tommy turns out to be a tough-minded but fair critic: "It ain't Willie, but it ain't bad at that. You know some more?"

Max is warmed up now and begins to use the table like a stage, working the audience that horseshoes around him. He does Roethke and Dylan Thomas and Housman. The beer is replaced by whiskey bought by Curly, who says no hard feelings about the elbow in his balls. Max has his foot to the floor now, redlining it, ad-libbing between the poems. He's sweating up there in the smoky light with a little blood caked around his nose, his eye squeezed shut and already going purple. They're clapping and cheering after each poem and I can see a few boots tapping along when Max leans into a rich iambic. He does two encores and then finishes with Yeats:

Heart-mysteries there and yet when all is said
It was the dream itself enchanted me . . .

Max is almost singing it now and I can see that it's not just the words, maybe hardly the words at all, but the current they generate that carries us along.

> . . . that raving slut
> Who keeps the till. Now that my ladder's gone,
> I must lie down where all the ladders start,
> In the foul rag-and-bone shop of the heart.

The bar is bedlam: hooting and piercing whistles and stomp-ing. Louise is up on the table wrapping Max up and leaning into a long, looping kiss. Curly pounds me on the back and someone is passing the hat. It comes back full of wrinkled bills, and Max, down from his perch, sets the hat on the bar and says we'll drink it dry. Tommy shakes his hand and apolo-gizes and someone gives him some ice wrapped in a bar towel for his eye. When Louise asks Max who wrote the poems, Max tells her he did.

"All the ones you liked anyway, honey. Why would I go around remembering what somebody else wrote?"

I can see that Louise is not too sure about this, so I ask her to dance. She wants to know what kind of guy Max really is and I tell her that I wouldn't even try to guess. After someone cuts in, I go back to the bar. Max's flush has faded and the jaundice he gets from drinking is starting to rise. I go to work on him, but it still takes me most of an hour to pry him loose. By then he's said a couple of things that could have been taken wrong ex-cept for all the sloshy goodwill.

Finally, there are good-byes all around. Curly asks Max his name and Max says it's Wallace Stevens. Then we're out in the dark, which nips me like a tonic. We walk around to where our car is, but instead of getting in Max opens the door of a pickup and hoists himself up so he's standing hunched in the door frame, holding himself there with one hand hooked around the back of the cab. I can't see what he's fooling around with in his other hand, and then he starts to recite "The Windhover." So I ask and he says whenever he can't get a stream started he recites Hopkins.

"If I want to puke, I do some late Auden."

What he's doing is pissing on the driver's seat. He gets three more trucks before I give up on talking him out of it and back the car out into the rutty lot. Max comes shambling then, stuffing himself back in, and even though a dog has started to bark I can see that we're going to get away without getting shot.

Max picks the back seat again. I've about run out of patience with myself because I can't begin to sort out how I feel about all this.

"They'll think twice about screwing with the next poet that comes along," says Max. He unlimbers a long, foggy belch and settles in. "And kid, let that be a lesson. If you want to grow up to be an artist, you can't ever let them get too familiar." Then he rumbles off to sleep.

And we're ninety miles out of Socorro, steady at eighty with all the windows down, taking our luck and chances down the road.

Going Away

As we begin our account it is June and Mr. Parker has come to Blueridge to salvage the accumulation of his life. The debris, as he puts it, of forty years. To accomplish this he carries a typewriter, four thousand dollars in traveler's checks, and his Navy trunk, dredged from the garage and packed sparingly. Travel light, travel far, Mr. Parker invents and the phrase lodges with him, inserting itself like a souvenir in conversations with himself.

Behind, Mr. Parker has left a divorce, a resignation. Husband, father, personnel systems response analyst, he has a citation for putting together a management package for the particleboard industry in China. And now he has come to Blueridge to assemble his life. Not *re*assemble, he insists in a draft of his first memo, for clearly it has never been intact. An easy judgment perhaps; common enough, certainly. In making it, Mr. Parker reveals to us much of his circumstance: drifting into his forties, he had come first to fear and then to believe that things which once mattered made no sense anymore, that the life he had arranged for himself was a pale fabrication, that he must achieve substance now or go to the grave a figment. He is not sure how true this is, but it seems true enough to act on. He leaves without telling anyone where he is going, without knowing himself. He chooses only not to leave the state. In some oblique way, that forestalls the sense of running away.

His wife was Barbara; his children, Stephanie, Scott, and Shannon. As an undergraduate, he once wrote half of what he explained was a Jamesian novel about growing up. For fifteen years, he has written only checks and memos. His wife writes all letters, even those to his parents. Now, with everything at stake, he begins again to write. He decides to call this material "memos." It is one of the few ironies he permits himself. For our purposes it is not necessary to know more. Except, perhaps, that he has just reread *Heart of Darkness*. This should afford us some perspective, some charity, in considering the psychological excess of his first memo.[1]

We may pass over this and future memos with little comment. They do, however, reveal of Mr. Parker a certain florid fluency which is less apparent in his conduct. This disparity narrows later, for we shall see language come to fail Mr. Parker as it becomes a more responsive image of its source.

He occupies the first afternoon in Blueridge writing and revising the memo. Finished, he is proud of its unsparing condemnations, its apocalyptic resolve. Later, when he reads it to the girl he will live with, she shrugs and says, "To thine own self . . . " It has always sounded like good advice to Mr. Parker. The girl adds, "And all that shit."

After supper Mr. Parker ponders between beginning some of Malcolm Lowry's late, long, redemptive stories and inves-

[1] I am forty-three years old. And I have learned that betrayal cores the heart of man. I would not claim this a contribution to human knowledge for we know it, all of us. But we remember, are called to acknowledge this, only as a collective accretion. Mass insanities of race, nation, or ideology— collective betrayal is plain, monstrous, and incalculable. It is this which enables us to assume some unspecifiable part as our responsibility and be done with it. For the ocean of such betrayal cannot be fathomed, and that which is not fathomable is not truly our own.

This much is clear. But it is not such betrayals which concern me here. Rather, it is a singular betrayal which I, full of misshapen notions of responsibility, created, nourished, sinewed into acts, and now must claim as my own. When I confess I am soul-sickened by the enormity of what I have done, I must insist that I speak as one who is rigorously descriptive. To judge this betrayal would be the most pedestrian exercise in irrelevance and worse. For judgment presumes to balance books, right scales, bring act and consequence into adjustment. It is the lackey of conscience, the refuge of those who feed their souls on the exceedingly fine grindings of the mills of morality.

No, judgment will not do. For I have relinquished my life. Faithful to the corrosive imperatives of the world, sucking the canker of comfort, I have sanitized those imperatives I suspected in myself. And I have come here, now, to resurrect those imperatives, redeem those betrayals, to find, if I dare, my own substance. The alternative to success in this is unthinkable.

tigating the local tavern. Isolation, he decides, will more likely make him a surly recluse than a saint.

The Firs is much like any beer bar in a small town in western Oregon. It contains a counter, stools, some cramped booths, a country-western jukebox, a shuffleboard and pool table, walls littered with signs and artifacts, linoleum floors, and smelly restrooms. A sign above the cash register reads "In God We Trust—All Others Pay Cash." The tavern is run by a genial owner and a divorced barmaid with two children. We detail it here because the Firs will become a landmark in Mr. Parker's new geography.

Mr. Parker, a gin-and-tonic man, remembers, coming through the door, how good beer used to be in college. He gets drunk and has a good time—losing at pool, losing at shuffleboard, winning the music at dice, throwing up when he gets back to his room. Travel light, travel far, he gurgles consolingly, hanging over the toilet.

In the morning Mr. Parker drives to the coast, gets sunburned, eats raw oysters, drives back at night with the windows open, sleeps till noon. When Mrs. Honnold asks how long he'll be staying, he gives her a month's rent.

Mr. Parker becomes a regular at the Firs. A bottle of Budweiser arrives without asking when he comes in. To nourish the beer-sloshed rapport with his new companions, he drives again to the coast, to Newport for a few days, learning to drink beer and shoot pool at some anonymous tavern. When he returns, he still loses, but not as badly.

His second memo follows the first by several weeks and is more temperate—though it deteriorates through several revisions. Its excesses are those we might expect in a man trying on new metaphors to accommodate beginnings.[2]

---

[2] It is imperative that a man be among men, and though lacking the substance that anchors and animates, I have found men to be among. They lack complex intelligence, clearly they are not entirely happy, yet I find them unmistakably human and that, first and finally, is what matters. They are hu-

Mr. Parker is encouraged by the speed and clarity of this recognition, but he has read enough to know that the motions of the heart are deceptive, to suspect the easy, the obvious. He would like to discover how they chose among possible selves, or whether they had to. Mr. Parker is not sure how to approach such questions. Instead, he asks about fishing and local history.

Although the blueprint of Mr. Parker's new architecture does not allow for it, he becomes aware of three women. Marge, the barmaid, is quick, bitter, and can land on her feet from any posture. May, an awesome drinker, is older and through three husbands. She contains a voluptuous pace, attractive to uncertain men. And Adrian. Almost a graduate of Mills College, she had lived in the Spanish Sahara for two years in hazy circumstances, had undertaken abortions in Mexico City, Gibraltar, and Oakland, and had come, amazingly, to Blueridge, for reasons similar to Mr. Parker's. She supports herself on the salary from a CETA job in which she is assembling an oral history of eastern Lane County.

Mr. Parker, sensing a new and vibrant sequence, participates with enthusiasm. Adrian is often lethargic, which encourages him to frisk outside his old protective reserve with women. In two weeks of beer and mutual confidings, both have talked out their histories. After such confidings there is nothing to do but live together.

They rent a small house west of town. The loggers, who have been unsuccessful with Adrian and have failed to penetrate the eager friendliness of Mr. Parker for an excuse to maul him, accept the situation much as they accept the fact that the Forest

---

man because they possess themselves. They do not relinquish the world, but the self is not derivative; it comes abundantly from inside. It is theirs. And it is right. And it is a large measure of what I seek. They have such limiting options, yet they have pursued selves as unique as fingerprints, true as carbon steel into old fir. I value them for this, and while I do not wish to imitate their forms, the true, tough fiber of their lives is the strength and substance which I seek.

Service, like rain down the backs of their necks, will be with them always. Their wives say occasionally vicious things about them at the laundromat, but they don't matter greatly, their role as moral arbiters lost back in the sixties.

After a month with Adrian, Mr. Parker is uneasy. His circumstances have altered substantially, but patterns remain unchanged. He continues to brush his teeth twice a day, he follows the baseball standings with interest, and he thinks about his past as much as ever. He drinks more now, but this was not really the sort of breakthrough he had in mind. His old self hunkers down, as if resolved to squat just out of reach until he resumes it. Perplexed, he reviews the memos to seek out how this has happened and what he might do differently. The memos, he decides, are ponderously pretentious, swollen by his inflated sense of self-magnitude in trying to remake his life. He resolves to write no more. Adrian goes to work haphazardly and is finally fired.

Through the summer they raise a garden, go fishing, smoke the marijuana that Adrian has and buy no more. Mr. Parker is glad. The smoke scours his throat, the effects are unnoticeable, and besides it's more or less illegal. Adrian moves on to herbal teas and tequila. His college alumni magazine finds him and he studies the class notes. He recognizes only a few of the names. Everyone is a success. Although he has never run before, Mr. Parker begins jogging. He quits after a week, unable to elude or pacify the town's dogs. They make love, of course, too. Mr. Parker devotes considerable energy to being mature and inventive. Adrian responds as conventionally as his wife.

They go to the ocean often. Watching the long swells come in, Adrian glazes over. At such times Mr. Parker wonders if she imagines herself a character in some foreign movie. Adrian will not admit it. Once, on the beach, Mr. Parker is sure he sees Shannon among a group of Girl Scouts. He maneuvers Adrian up toward the high tide line, rummaging through driftwood until the girls have passed.

Adrian does not speak of her family, but once some friends come through from California. They have three large dogs: Earth, Kilo, and Hoist. One is an Afghan, the other two are indecipherable. Mr. Parker cannot remember the friends' names. They sleep out front in a Volkswagen bus with West Virginia plates and eat ravenously. Mr. Parker is polite, the friends are polite. They have nothing to say to each other. After a week they leave for British Columbia.

By September Mr. Parker is going to the bar, nightly, alone. His companions there have become predictable, their self-hood nothing more than the drudge of routine. He feels cheated, but is not sure how or by whom. Whenever possible he drinks by himself. Adrian reads Joyce Carol Oates, writes letters, goes to bed early. Mr. Parker has never read Joyce Carol Oates. He finds her at first disturbing, then repetitive. He does not say so. When the rains start in November, Mr. Parker, depressed, is ready. They confirm his developing belief that life moves in dismal cycles, tending always towards winter.

In December, three days before his anniversary, Mr. Parker explains he has business with his bank. The lie animates him for several days, but Adrian doesn't notice. He drives to Portland, parks in a downtown garage, rents another car, and drives past his home three times. The Buick is in the driveway, along with a car he doesn't recognize. The house has been painted a different color. When he calls later from a bar, ready to disguise his voice, not knowing what he will say, no one is home.

Adrian is asleep when he returns. After he has persistently touched her awake, she says it is her period and asks him to rub her back.

She leaves in December, a week before Christmas. Mr. Parker returns from the bar one afternoon and she is gone. He is stricken with an urgent sense of relief. Travel light, travel far, he repeats giddily, dusting shelves, changing sheets, cleaning the bathroom.

He goes home that night with Marge, marveling at such quick luck. He wakes once at the sound of a pickup, certain one of the loggers will come through the door and hit him in the stomach before he can get his pants on. In the morning he rises before the others and fixes breakfast. The two children pour sugar on the table, spill milk, and the boy tells Marge to fuck herself when she slaps him for neglecting his burned eggs.

Mr. Parker goes home, sleeps, goes out, buys a bottle, comes home, and writes the last memo we shall consider here.[3] If we detect an aroma of desperation, it is because Mr. Parker is getting scared.

The winter is tenacious. Mr. Parker invents a letter. The rain, he will write, grows moss on his soul. He suffers the bucolic plague. If death consumes us all, what's left but life? He cannot think of anyone to send the letter to.

By March Mr. Parker has three hundred dollars and the rent is due. Although he lives frugally, eating little, the beer and a quart of gin, drunk straight, every three and a half days, have depleted him. Adrian has depleted him. There is no call here for personnel systems response analysts, but leaving Blueridge for such a place has never been admissible.

The rain stops early. Mr. Parker buys jeans, boots, gloves, suspenders, and tries three logging companies. He had set chokers one summer during college. But the woods are tight, real loggers are out of work. Mr. Parker thinks this is bad luck for him. It is not.

The other employer in Blueridge is the Forest Service. Mr. Parker takes a Civil Service exam and watches his money recede. His score, finally, is the second highest ever recorded on the Blueridge Ranger District. Sized up as too old for stren-

---

[3]   I   I must act to change my understanding.
    II   I must try to understand my acts.
    III   I must convert my acts to change.
    IV   Trying to convert my understanding, I must change my act.

uous fieldwork, he is offered a job as a lookout. In early June the Forest Service packer hauls him in to Walker Mountain.

Straddling a divide between the McKenzie and Willamette drainages, commanding a view of rich timber country and a large chunk of wilderness to the east, Walker Mountain is one of the few manned lookouts remaining in the Cascades. It can be reached by trail and by Forest Service radio. At that elevation, in that solitude, the radio sounds like the voice of God.

Ninety feet up in the tower, storing supplies, Mr. Parker discovers a note left by his immediate, perhaps his only, predecessor. The packer has said that Frank was on the mountain every summer for thirty-seven years. The note, printed carefully across the top of a fire sighting form, is written in fierce red ink: "The roof leaks over the stove."

After a week Mr. Parker has called in two controlled slash burns, smoke from the Pope & Talbot mill, a campfire at the Stony Meadow Recreation Site, and a pocket of fog on upper Piecemeal Creek. He can't understand much of what goes on over the radio and he no longer wears clothes. Travel light, travel far, he says, cleaning the tower's windows with his underwear.

Once a month the packer brings food, a paycheck, company. The packer drinks hugely and will talk all night about fires.

Mr. Parker begins to experiment. Dry needles, cones, bark, dead manzanita and fern. He keeps a record of how they ignite, burn, go out. The packer brings stubby candles and he tests them too. Once, just before dark, an owl flies into the glass. Mr. Parker, studying maps, lurches up, terrified. That night he bolts the door. In the morning the owl is gone from the walkway.

By September Mr. Parker is ready. He has begun jogging again, plodding along the trail to his lookout, and can run four miles without stopping. He also has a potato sack of cedar needles and dried manzanita leaves, twenty candles, and a well-marked map.

The burning index rises and stays high. College begins and the summer help quits, leaving the fire crews depleted. He waits for an east wind, and it comes. The forest is closed, logging shut down. The Forest Service, the Governor, everybody declares a fire emergency. On the radio the Blueridge Fire Control Officer exhorts Mr. Parker to watch relentlessly. Mr. Parker promises.

That night he finds Frank's note and prints beneath it: "The floor leaks under the stove." He does not know if this is true, but it seems probable. Leaving the lookout, hiking hard, he sets candles and kindling at the base of steep east slopes, in roadless country, visible only from his lookout.

Two days later he is done, watching smoke from his second fire swell into the sky miles away. Four of his fires go, two don't. They are controlled after burning twenty thousand acres. Mr. Parker hikes out, boards a Greyhound in Crescent, heads south. Travel light, travel far, he repeats. He is no longer sure what this means, but it seems a familiar comfort. He is not surprised when the FBI arrests him at the Sacramento depot.

His divorce becomes final during the trial, where psychiatrists alternately declare him accountable and unaccountable for burning up 130,000,000 board feet of Willamette National Forest timber. Some come from Blueridge to testify, Adrian cannot be found, his family stays away. The federal prosecutor introduces the kindling notes, left at the lookout, as evidence of his intelligence, rationality, purpose. The less lucid memos seem to have vanished.

Mr. Parker, having neither explanation nor remorse, has no defense. In court, he is congenial to everyone but otherwise takes little interest in the case. After presentence investigation, he receives three years for arson. His attorney is outraged. Mr. Parker refuses to allow an appeal to be filed.

In prison he is inconspicuous and enjoys the small privileges of inmates who are not criminals. He begins what he describes as a Kafkaesque novel about growing up and after a year assumes editorship of the prison newspaper. In national competition with weekly papers published at institutions of more than five hundred but fewer than a thousand inmates, it receives third place. His own column, "Convictions," is singled out for special mention.

So we have encountered Mr. Parker, followed his horizontal progress, and now must pass on to other matters. But what are we to make of this? Surely, the seeking of a better self engages our best wishes and support. Aberrations in pursuit of that self provide a certain interest. Adrian, Blueridge, the family are admittedly pallid, but that is not our concern. And the memos, once promising, serve in the end, as does most language, the prosecuting attorneys of our world. How, then, account to the worm of consequence for time spent here?

A possibility reveals itself and I will advance it, enforce it even. We may leave our fiction, exiting through one of Mr. Parker's recent columns: "Only this: That the world is a hard place for us all, that resolve to change our lives is seldom enough, that damaged men, grounded in blundering circumstance, merit neither compassion nor lament but human affirmation as one of us—all of us. We must believe this, we must believe this I swear it, or we can believe nothing else again."

Waterworks, Rim, and Angel

though they were mirrors. You may recall the mishap that closed his career in this world.)

You must think me quite mad, of course, but when has madness been an impediment to government service? In any event, such judgement is a ludic irrelevance below the Rim. This Station is my charge, not from political hacks but from the Angel Himself. (I mention the Angel only by way of assurance that I have not taken this matter into my own hands; I am in His governance absolutely.)

Although I trust the Angel impeccably, I have found it prudent to take certain mundane precautions. Should memory balk, your files will remind you of my gift for undoing: precisely, my military service in the Pacific Theatre with a specialization in demolitions. While you must understand that I cannot be more specific, you should know that any attempt to interfere with my work will assure the absolute razing of the powerhouse & the conclusive loss of your water source. Do not mistake me. Roughly adjusted for inflation, we're talking about 11 million dollars, give or take. A sum sufficient to attract the attention of the Secretary himself, I should think.

With respect to fiscal matters, you may feel free to suspend my stipend. I require only my semi-annual provisionment. (I take this occasion to supplement the list I sent out last month with the packer: 50' of 20-gauge 6" stainless steel pipe; 2 doz. hex head 4" lag bolts; 5 lbs. corn starch; 10 lbs. aluminum rivets; 200 lbs. quicklime; 1 case My-Tee-Fine peaches in syrup; 5 gal. 90 wt. gear oil; 200' of #10 double insulated wire; a list of all previous winners of the Nobel Prize in metaphysics.)

Let me anticipate here your argument that this matter is out of your hands as well—that even should you accept my terms, your superiors would have none of it. I am certain, first, that you have not risen so far in the federal trade without developing such skills as would permit you to explain me to or conceal me from whatever superiors must be tended to. I would also relate an anecdote, a cautionary tale, if you will, that concerns one of your antecedents in the superintendency & may prove instructive to yourself. The man (on principle, I do not perpetuate the names of fools) came to the persuasion that an automated Station would enhance matters. I mistakenly allowed this equipment to be installed, though you may be certain that I registered the strongest possible objections. The arrogance of such machinery was a sacrilege here (like the rubbish that goes up & down the trail, interfering with my work). Of course, it failed. How could it do otherwise with no one to intercede, to, shall we say, make proper arrangements with the Angel?

The story goes on to acquire a certain satisfying symmetry. Subsequent to this incident, the man's firstborn arrived with a withered digit, his wife made off with a vigorous environmentalist & the man himself developed shingles. His next—& I have no reason to doubt, last—post was as curator of the Millard Fillmore National Historical Site.

There are causes, sir, things in this world that are better left alone. Your perspective & therefore your authority end at the Canyon's edge. Beneath the Rim, the authority of eternity holds. It is this power that I serve in serving the Angel.

You are concerned, of course, with the future: who, you may ask, will one day replace me? This is not your concern. The Angel bore me here, as He did my forerunner, as He will my successor.

I have laboured to account for the Angel's interest in such machinery. But theology is the world's work (& the Devil's, if I may say so), words carpentered to house what even this Canyon cannot contain. The luminous offers no account: its terms are unconditional & untranslatable.

I trust I have been perfectly clear. Now that you understand what is necessary, there is no need for further exchange between us.

Respectfully yrs,

Samuel Eisenbrock, Tender
Bright Angel Station

The Lord of Misrule at Separation Creek

On the west slope of the Oregon Cascade Mountains, deep inside the Three Sisters Wilderness, Separation Creek rises on the flank of the South Sister and flows west and north some twenty miles into Horse Creek. It is an ordinary stream, bright as ice and dropping steeply once it leaves the high meadow country. It had been called Whistling Jesus Creek by settlers after a circuit-riding preacher whose cabin stood near the stream's mouth. The name was changed with the coming of the U.S. Forest Service and the federal tidying up of bawdy or otherwise unsuitable place names.

Some few years ago, a party traveling north from Sphinx Butte broke out of heavy timber into Separation Meadow on the afternoon of the summer solstice. The group numbered perhaps a dozen, more women than men, and was led by a stocky man with a sprightly stride. They moved into the meadow, following the man toward a stand of pine, aspen, and spruce which covered a little rise in the grassy plain. The party was variously dressed, but the stocky man's cobalt shirt and lemon pants lit the meadow like a burning shrub. All carried heavy packs which they shrugged off clumsily when the buoyantly dressed man stopped at the verge of the rise.

They sank down beside the packs, but their leader, after scanning the meadow, walked on into the trees. Some time later he rejoined the group and spread his arms in wide embrace, facing east across the brilliant meadow towards the rising forest and the great snowy volcanoes of the Cascade summit.

A bright cheer rose from the group, and people began breaking out their gear. By late afternoon, tents bloomed at the edge of the rise, and the party was busy embellishing their campsite. Streamers, wind chimes, and globes of colored glass were hung from trees and from a network of lines run among the trees. Balloons were filled from a small tank and tied in clusters, and in the meadow ingenious miniature windmills were assembled, their vermilion and copper blades flashing as wind riffled the grassy flat. Bits of mirror and colored glass were tacked up on trees or wedged in the crotch of branches. One woman launched six kites, each resembling a different exotic beast. Through the afternoon, a storehouse of wood was gathered. The men dragged and rolled great logs to the pile and built a fire ring with stones carried from the creek.

The leader sat far out in the flat, facing away from the group, until the afternoon light thickened towards sunset. He swept up then and came across the meadow, gesturing like a mime, his face painted in an exaggerated mask of delight. Reaching the group, he bantered away questions, teasing the women and joking with the men. He sent the men away for more wood and settled around the cooking fire with the women, helping to prepare the evening meal, a richly spiced stew.

After supper the stained-glass lanterns were lit. Across the meadow the silver light drained away into the surface of Separation Creek. The man ignited the main fire, adding wood until it blazed up as high as his shoulders. He stepped back deliberately, thirty paces or so; then, with a yip of glee, he broke into a run towards the fire. Nearly there, he flung himself through three handsprings before vaulting in a double flip across the flames. Landing, the man spread his arms, palms up, and bowed to the applause. From a leather pouch on his belt, he drew out a bell and rang it crisply. At the sound each member of the group clasped his own hands, as if greeting himself.

"There is a place in the high desert, east of the Steens Mountains in the Alvord Basin. Gypsum flats, briny seeps, hot springs. Some alkaline lakes. Plants do not grow there; even the weather seems a stranger. But there are creatures here that are rare—rare and wonderful. A tusked fish that burrows into the sulfury mud. Blind, albino lizards far back in the basaltic caves. Carnivorous moths. I have seen these things." The man sprang into a back flip, and the people let go of their hands and rang bells like the one the man carried.

"My friends, are you less rare? The ordinary world has made

you. So what? It has made you and made you and one day it must destroy you for being what it made. This is complicated and it is not fair and it fills us with fear." The man vaulted in front of the fire again, his face stretched like a tragic mask, and a moaning passed among the people.

"Therefore, everyone wants to save you. Everyone says: 'Change and you will be saved.' But I say to you, if you want to change go away from us." The man's arms flared out. "Here, I give you permission to be. I allow, I permit, I enable only one thing: that you be. Here you strip off all that encumbers, cast away old changes until you reach the pure vein, the pure joy that is your first self."

The bells pealed out across the meadow where nighthawks wheeled through the insect nations. The man dropped down, then pressed into a handstand, making one circuit of the fire before he resumed.

"Oh, the lords of law," the man said, his voice a husky whisper. "The masters of propriety, of discipline, of family. The grim captains of the church and the university and the marketplace. The magistrates of the superego and the Other. The lords of demand steal you away from your first self. You ask me who I am, and I tell you now, have brought you here to tell you." His voice rose out of him now like molten amber.

"I am the Lord of Misrule. I throw over the lords of rule and set you free."

The next morning the man led the band to the bank of a grassy oxbow of Separation Creek. He asked each one to call up some moment from his past, cup it in his hands, then sluice them through the flowing water.

"The lords of rule bind you with the past and the future. Only the present sets you free. Your past flushes out of your hands; your future sweeps away in the current and no man can know it. When your hands are no longer full of the past and the future, you may hold the present in them. You may hold a life which is your own."

Each morning at the oxbow the man repeated these words. At night before the fire, expansive and acrobatic, he amplified the doctrine. Sometimes he juggled as he spoke, weaving arcs with blue and lime and burgundy balls that glowed faintly in the dark.

"This is, all of it, about joy. If I ever grow too heavy you must remind me. Ring the small bells, the little tinklers.

"As you draw near to your first self you will shiver in delight, go blind with joy.

"You can see that I want nothing from you. Let us be candid. Not money, not sex, not power. It is my gift: I offer your lives to you."

As the summer deepened, the man taught each of them a different acrobatic stunt. Whenever they performed the routine, he said, they were leaving their old bodies behind. Most had little talent for such feats, but several women and one bantamweight man grew quite fluent.

The man set them other tasks as well. Some involved patterns of eating and defecation, about which the man had a great store of riddles and puns. There was also a daily walk-about during which each member of the band went farther into the wilderness, leaving behind some small possession and returning with a piece of wood to be added to the effigy that was constructed during the week. At week's end, the man placed an article of his own on the effigy and it was burned. And in all of this, the man insisted that they hold always before them their purpose: to strip away the overburden, turning over the layers of not-you until they struck the true ore of the self.

In late August two men slipped away with no explanation. Not long after, a woman, whose behavior had become increasingly erratic, stormed off after a dispute about the lyrics of a Cat Stevens song. The man was disconsolate, hunched in the meadow all one day until the group surrounded him at dusk, ringing the tiny bells that sprung him into a goofy ragman dance which everyone joined. That night, he brought out the tank of nitrous oxide.

As the light tarnished towards autumn, the encampment took on the sadness of debris and things too long in the weather. Charred wood lay about the fire rings built near each tent. Tinfoil and shreds of plastic and scraps of parachute cord were scattered across the packed dirt of the cooking area, and bits of soiled tissue blew about. The kites had been torn away in a fierce and sudden wind that had left the streamers in tatters and uprooted the windmills. Bits of mirror and colored glass still glinted richly in the trees, but on the ground beneath, the tents were streaked and faded. The grassy soil of the oxbow had been beaten down into hardpan, and chunks of the bank had sloughed off where the group came down to flush their hands each morning. As the people came and went across the meadow, their trails deepened into ruts.

Their leader bore them above all of this, buoying the group with laughter and promise and forgetfulness.

"What we do here, remember, is peculiar. To take back your life from the hands of others is peculiar. To invent the present each day is peculiar. You must always surprise yourself; only in surprise and laughter are you free."

Two days before the equinox, the man directed that a feast be prepared from the remaining stores. The next morning in a great patchwork cloak he led the group in serpentine procession to the creek. Dressed in their brightest clothes, bells chiming in the crisp air, they wove through the meadow downstream from the oxbow where Separation Creek pooled behind a small logjam.

"You have scrubbed away the past and have forsaken the future. Still, there is one more thing. The last thing you must cast away is myself."

Distressed murmurs rose up from the people. The man waved them to silence.

"It is the right thing, you shall see. But first we must celebrate the self you have recovered. We must crystallize it in these waters; then travel over the crest and confirm it in the twin waters of the other side."

As he spoke, the man stepped apart from the group. His arms began to shovel air, and bruise-colored smoke rolled from his fingertips.

"The Lord of Misrule commands you: each of you now make a joyful run and extravagant leap into these waters." Each did, as the tang of smoke rode on the air and the man crinkled in laughter. When everyone was in the stream, the man snapped his fingers out and somersaulted into the pool, inciting a magnificent water fight.

Later, around the fire, the man explained what remained to be done. The next day, on the equinox, he would lead them across the pass between the Middle and South Sister. On the other side they would repeat their celebration in Blockhouse Creek. Then they must drive him away.

The next morning the band set out east across the meadow. Their leader carried a pack with provisions for an evening meal after the ceremony. Everything else was left behind. Pockets of ground fog hung in the meadow, and their pants were soaked with dew before they reached the timber.

By afternoon they were above timberline. Someone had wrenched an ankle crossing a patch of scree and had dropped behind with a companion. The rest went on up to a small cinder cone not far below the pass itself. By the time the stragglers had caught up, weather was rolling in from the southwest, already past Diamond Peak and careening along the crest.

The man urged them up, miming a frantic conductor making ready the departure of a train. Laughing, they rose and climbed on. Again, the same pair dropped back and were already out of sight of the rest when the rain struck. Within minutes snow was falling, driven in wild swarms by the wind. The man gathered the group and told them they must keep moving. The pass, he said, was near, and the storm might beat itself out on this side of the summit. He approached each of them, rubbing their cheeks until the friction warmed them. Then he sprang ahead into the spreading snow.

Near dusk the man came through the pass and, dropping down a few hundred feet, left the storm above him. At timberline he built a great fire and waited.

Behind, blinded in the snow and oncoming dark, the band had separated into two groups with several lone stragglers. Some continued to climb; others felt their way downslope. Here and there bells rang out, the sound torn away in the roaring wind.

Two of the group made it down to the rain and the sheltering timber that night. One more came down the next morning. They rested a day at the encampment, eating a stash of licorice that one of them had left on a walkabout. The next day they hiked out to the Frog Camp trailhead.

It took the search party several days to find all the bodies. Two of them were frozen in grotesque acrobatic contortions. Another had a small bell clenched in her teeth.

Before the long snows reached Separation Meadow, a Forest Service packer and trail crew came in and cleaned out the encampment, burning what debris they could and packing out the rest on the mules.

On the tenth anniversary of the deaths, a staff writer for *Pacific Rim* magazine tracked down the leader of the group. His name was Jerry Corbet. He was director of recreation for a small chain of nursing homes in the mid-South. After the deaths, he had gone to the sheriff's office. They had taken his statement, but there was nothing to charge him with. The statement remained sealed, and Corbet left the state.

Corbet reluctantly agreed to an interview on the condition that his location not be divulged. He had little to tell the writer. Corbet refused to discuss his purposes in forming the group, except to say that recent medical research had confirmed the therapeutic effects of laughter. The writer prodded Corbet for an account of his actions during the storm and received an uninflected summary. When Corbet reached the pass, he waited. After no one came, he crossed over and built a signal fire. He stayed there through the night and into the next afternoon. By then it was apparent, he said, that everyone had chosen to return to the encampment, so he hiked out.

Corbet indicated that he was married, but would not say whether he had children. He said that the episode was not a part of his life that he dwelled on. At the end of the interview, he agreed to be photographed facing away from the camera in a handstand.

After a few summers, the meadow and grove were much as they had always been. Separation Creek carved a sharp, new bank in the oxbow, and saplings grew out of the mossy fire rings. Here and there, though, bits of colored glass remain, mostly now in the nests of Steller's Jays, those disorderly harlequins of the high country.

Christmas at
the Dixie Motel

"I won't do anything right away, but I'm not going to just let it pile up. The girls' needs are the same, whether you're working or not."

"Sure," I say. Katy and Gretchen are already in the room fiddling with the television. The street is gray slush—matches the Wisconsin sky—but it's Sunday afternoon and there's only the tracks of my car and Carla's in the motel lot.

"If I have to I'll take it to court. I promise you, they don't fool around up here."

"I'll bet they don't. This is such a wholesome state, I'm amazed they let anyone get divorced at all."

Carla almost bites before she remembers she doesn't need to anymore.

"I'll be at work, so call my mother if something comes up."

She looks pretty good all bundled up; you can't tell her weight thirty pounds one way or the other. In Houston, too much of her showed. Up here when everyone finally unwraps from the winter, Carla blends right in. I think if Carla had been skinnier and we'd had air conditioning in the car, she never would have left. She sees it a little different, of course.

So far we've both been pretty cordial, considering. I tap on the window and she rolls it down a couple of inches. I can see her motivational cassettes on the dash.

"Merry Christmas," I say. "Come by for some eggnog."

"Jesus, Roy." She rolls the window up and backs out.

"There's no cable here, Dad."

"This is my bed."

"I'm not sleeping with her; she still pees her pants."

"No I don't."

I wrestle them both to the bed and growl like a bear.

"Dad, you're messing up my hair."

"Katy pees her hair."

"You're dumb. Nobody can do that."

"Hey," I say, "let's get a Christmas tree."

It's late when I finally find the place. I want to get a cut-your-own tree because that's how we did it before we moved to Texas. Gretchen doesn't want to get out of the car. Katy sees a tree she likes and I saw it off.

"Remember when we did this out in the woods, in Oregon?"

"No. Did I have fun?"

"You bet."

I wedge the tree in the trunk and climb in. Gretchen is crying.

"She did it, Dad. Evidently, you should have made her go when we stopped."

"I can't open the door." Gretchen cries and stutters.

Katy starts to chip in again and I tell her to lighten up, that Gretchen is only four.

"Yeah, lighten up," says Gretchen, still hiccuping. Katy clams up in a sulk and stays clammed up as I get the car stuck turning around. When it's clear that I'm not going to get it out, I start swearing and hit the dash a couple of times with my open hand.

"Daddy, that makes me scared."

The man who owns the tree lot comes back with me in his pickup. I crawl under the front end and hook a chain on and he pulls me out.

"Don't see much snow in Texas, I expect."

My jeans are soaked through and my knuckles are scuffed and greasy.

"Sure don't," I say, chipper as I can. "What do I owe you?"

"Fifteen for the tree; another fifteen for the tow ought to make it right."

I give him the money, but I can't quite leave it alone.

"You do a pretty good business in the swamp back here?"

"What are you getting at?"

And then I leave it alone.

"Merry Christmas."

In the little hubbub, I get away with his saw.

It's dark on the way back and we're picking up some sleet. I make Katy turn the radio off so I can concentrate on the road. I miss the freeway turnoff anyway and have to pick my way back on the side streets. The car is toasty now, topped off with a sniff of urine that comes and goes.

"Will you ever forget who I am?" asks Gretchen.

The tree stays in the trunk overnight. I promise decorations and presents tomorrow, sealing the deal with a delivered pizza. I turn on the shower and herd them into the bathroom. Gretchen peels right down, but Katy hesitates. I find something to do in the other room. She's nine years old; we haven't lived together for two years. Is it OK for me to see her without any clothes on? Am I supposed to feel like some gawky stranger, into whose hands my children have fallen?

"Easy does it, pal," I say out loud. "Eat your heart out on your own time." That sounds kind of catchy, and I wonder if I've heard it somewhere before. A woman I know says country and western songs got her through every major crisis in her life.

When they're tucked in with the pizza and some fuzzy movie, I nip next door to Dan's Discount Liquors. The vodka is almost twice what it costs in Houston, but I buy a bottle anyway and something to drink it with. Easy does it, I think on the way back. I've had some trouble with the stuff off and on. I can't say that it didn't have something to do with Carla bailing out, but the last year we were together I hardly touched it. Even when I drank, I didn't get stopped for DWI and I never hit her although once I nailed all the doors shut when she was at one of her $200 get-togethers where you find out that you're the only thing holding yourself back. I wait till the girls are asleep to break out the bottle.

A mailman is whistling down the street in the movie.

"Do you know him?" Gretchen asks.

"Dad doesn't work for the Post Office. He works for United Package Service."

"Parcel Service," I say.

"What's the difference?"

"Not much. I guess they think parcel sounds better."

"Isn't Christmas pretty busy? Don't they need you?"

"Not right now."

"Why not?"

I can see Dan's sign flashing through a gap in the curtain.

"It's sort of complicated."

"Did you get fired?"

"Is that what your mother says?"

"No."

"What does she say?"

"She never says anything about you."

That night Gretchen wets the bed and then climbs in with me. Katy has one leg hanging out, she's over so far to keep from touching the wet spot, so I get her in with us too. Carla nursed them both and sometimes she'd fall asleep and I'd worry that one of us would roll over on them, but of course we never did. Now they claim their space in the bed like veterans. In the morning, we do a round robin back scratch although Gretchen doesn't want to do much scratching. She pushes at my hairline.

"Daddy, your forehead got bigger."

"Daddy's getting smarter, that's why."

"Evidently, Uncle Ralph must be the smartest man in the world." Katy has inherited my sense of humor. I bury her face with a pillow and do my growl. Uncle Ralph is a jerk and bald as a brick.

Every morning we have breakfast at McDonald's. Sometimes I see women with their kids, but I never see another father, not even on the weekend. Katy knows the way to the mall, and I buy more presents than I'd meant to. I can drive back to Houston on plastic. We get some ornaments and two strings of lights. At the last minute, Katy remembers a stand for the tree. I say it's only going to be up a couple of days—we can rig something or lean it in a corner, but she really wants a stand we can put water in so we get one.

The tree doesn't look half bad when we're finished. We've scooted the bed back to make room for it in front of the window. I've broken off some of the low branches so the presents will fit. Katy tries to make a wreath with them, but we don't have the right stuff. Finally, we drape them on top of the curtain rod.

We should be outside more, but I don't much want to drive and there aren't any sidewalks out here. The bathroom has a little porthole window, and when I go in to take a leak I pull back the plastic curtain. There's about ten feet between the motel and a chain link fence. The snow isn't that deep, but it's not trampled up, just the usual city scum on the top. I bundle us all up and we go around back to make a snowman. The balls pick up gravel and weeds when we roll them. By mashing them into the fence, I can make it more interesting. I build arms so the snowman looks like he's flexing. Gretchen plops a snowball-sized bicep on.

"He's got big muscles, just like Stan."

"Who's Stan?"

"Nobody," says Katy quickly.

Across the fence is a loading dock for some kind of sheet metal shop. And all of a sudden on the roof of the building, standing next to the edge and looking not down but off in the distance somewhere is a goat.

"Hey, look at that," I say. "It's a goat."

"Wow," says Gretchen.

"Evidently, it's a mountain goat," says Katy.

But it's not. It's just your basic barnyard nanny, the kind that used to keep down the blackberry vines and poison oak in Oregon about three lifetimes ago.

It's only a one-story building, but it's still twenty feet or so to the ground and the goat isn't about to jump. We follow the fence around front but the gates are locked. I can't tell whether the place is closed for the holidays or out of business.

"I'll call the animal people, or the police."

"How do you think he got up there?"

"I don't know. Maybe he's a watchgoat."

"Dad."

"Or maybe Santa's using goats this year instead of reindeer."

"Daddy, no he doesn't."

"One time when I was out looking for arrowheads, I saw a mountain lion on a ledge about that far above me."

"Wow," says Gretchen. "What's a mountain lion?"

"You already told us about that," says Katy.

When they're settled in with the afternoon cartoons, I walk down to the office. I ring the bell and after a little bit I hear a couple of locks click.

"You want something?" The manager is about my age, but he's got a bunch of miles on me.

"I need to use the phone."

He slips the door chain and opens up.

"I guess I need a phone book too."

He finds one in a stack behind the counter.

"Local calls are fifty cents a pop; no long distance except collect."

The plastic centerpiece on the phone says "Dixie Motel." Underneath, the number reads VIctory 4-5333.

I call the Humane Society and tell them about the goat. They're skeptical, but they want to know where it is. The manager doesn't know what the place is called. We play a little game of ask-the-right-question and it turns out to be the forty-five thousand block of Fond du Lac. The Humane Society promises to check it out.

"That on the level?"

I've hung up, and I'm fishing in my pocket for fifty cents.

"Sure," I say. I put two quarters on the counter.

"Skip it."

"Think your boss can afford it?"

"I'm the boss."

"While I'm here, I need a change of sheets."

He gives me a look that says I'm pushing my luck.

"Ninety-five a week don't include laundry. If you wanted that, you should have said so."

"So I'm saying so. How much for a couple of sheets?"

"And I ought to charge you the electric if you're going to keep those Christmas lights on."

It's the holiday season, I say to myself; everybody wants to be Santa Claus. He goes into the back and comes out with two sheets. One has "Super 8 Motel" stenciled on it.

"How much?" I say.

He plops them on the linoleum counter.

"Want a drink?"

I discover that I do. We go back into his living quarters. The place is about twice the size of my room, which isn't much, and it's a bunker. Not *like* a bunker. I know; I've spent some time in them. He's got sandbags stacked up six feet high all around the walls and there's enough weaponry for a platoon. He pours us each a glass of bourbon and we sit at the kitchen table. I wonder how you casually ask somebody why his living room looks like the DMZ. One thing's for sure: I'm not going to make any jokes. But I don't have to. He waves his hand.

"The deal is," he says, "is they're taking over motels all over the country. I didn't spend two years fighting gooks to have them come over here and overrun everything. They're in for a little surprise when they come for the Dixie."

"I can see that."

"Wally," he says, and reaches out.

"Roy."

"That your real name?"

"Sure," I say, "why not?"

"Around here, I figure I get about fifty/fifty."

The bourbon is really bad, but I sip enough to be polite.

"That broad out there the other day, she your ex?"

I shake my head yes.

"Tough luck."

I'm not sure how he means it, so I just agree.

After a bit, I tell him I better be getting back to the girls. Wally gets up too.

"I just thought of something."

He walks me down to the end room. It costs too much to heat, so he uses it for storage. He goes through some boxes and finally pulls out one of those $5.98 hard plastic dolls you get at Kmart.

"Somebody left this." He holds it out to me.

"Thanks."

"You want another drink, drop by."

"Thanks. I'm kind of trying to lay off the stuff."

"I hear you, brother."

The doll has a crack across her head and something crusted on her dress. I take it in under my coat. When we go out for supper, I slip it in the trash at Burger King.

The girls pester me about what the presents are and about opening some early. Two more days, I say. We'll do it the night before I leave. They tickle me, but I don't crack.

"I want you to live with me, Daddy."

"So you can tickle me all the time?"

"No. I want you to live with me. Why don't you live with me?"

"Because your mother has a gizzard where her heart is supposed to be."

"What's a gristle?"

"Dad, want to play Yahtzee?"

It's true, but I shouldn't say it; they're her kids too.

"Your mother and I didn't get along."
Gretchen lights up.
"Daddy, I know; you could ride in the back seat."

After the girls are asleep, I have some vodka to settle my stomach from the bourbon and onion rings. I sort of let things happen, and pretty soon it all washes back up again. For the first year or so, I'd make up ways they'd come back. They'd show up out of nowhere on Thanksgiving. Or Carla would be crippled in a wreck or get breast cancer and I'd take her back anyway. Sometimes I'd imagine doing something heroic that she'd see on the news. I even thought about grabbing the girls and running. One time all this got mixed up with the real world. Carla's Catholic, so when the Pope came I drove out to San Antonio. I guess I thought something might happen, even though I'm not Catholic or any sort of Christian to speak of. They had an outdoor Mass west of the city; there must have been a quarter of a million people. I saw him up close in that two-story rig he rides around in. It turns out he's kind of dinky. At the end when people lined up all over the hillside for Communion, I figured I'd better too if anything was going to come of it. The woman giving out the stuff was dressed just like everybody else. She said "Body of Christ" to me but she didn't give me the cracker, like I was supposed to say something back or she could tell that I wasn't really Catholic. Then she gave it to me and I ate it, but of course nothing happened.

I remember to wake Gretchen up and put her on the can. We wait a while.
"I can't go."
"That's OK, dumpling." I lift her off.
"What's the dumpling?"
"Something good to eat." I make little smacking noises at the back of her neck.
"You smell funny, Daddy."

I look out through the curtain. A man has just come from the office. He parks his car and gets out with a woman and they go into a room. It's been snowing again. I wonder what the roads are going to be like in two days going south.

Sometimes I think she left because her father died when she was thirteen. You don't have to be a shrink to know that no husband is ever going to measure up to a thirteen-year-old girl's father. And sometimes I think it was all that death: her father, the two abortions that I know of, the boyfriend she probably would have married killed in a car wreck. Except for Carla, I'm the only one who knows. And now I'm dead.

There's not enough left to be worth saving, so I pour myself the rest of the vodka. I'll have to remember to take some aspirin before I go to sleep. I cup my hands around my face and blow, but I can't tell if I smell funny. I lean over Gretchen and sniff. I thought there might be some of that old warm, sleepy baby smell. Instead, she smells like a shower is first thing up in the morning. Since I'm at it, I sniff at Katy's face. She smells like a person. I'm sorry about a lot of things. One is telling Carla that sometimes she smelled like bad fish. Maybe it was the humidity.

In the whole thing, the only time I cried was after we'd separated. It was before she moved to Wisconsin. I talked her into a weekend at Corpus without the kids. I don't know why she came; like she said, it only complicated things. It was a little funny, dating your own wife, but it got better as it went along and I even got her to laughing. I had to promise there wouldn't be any sex, but the second night I started fooling around and she didn't stop me. Things went along, but nothing was happening for me and then she was ready and I couldn't do it. She tried a couple of things, but they didn't work. After a while she patted my cheek and took a blanket and slept on the couch. That was the first time that had happened to me except once or twice when I was drunk. All of a sudden I was crying and I couldn't stop, even though I knew she could hear me. They moved to Wisconsin a couple months later.

CHRISTMAS AT THE DIXIE MOTEL

I see that the snow has stopped. The car that came in is gone and the lights in the office are out. The room is warmer tonight, and I wonder if Wally turned up the heat for us. When I told my mother about the divorce, my father came on the phone, which he never does.

"Did you beat her up or step out on her?"

"No, Dad."

"Well why, then?"

"She wanted something else."

"You mean somebody can get a divorce just because they don't want to be married anymore?"

"That's right, Dad."

"Well no goddamn wonder there's so much of it."

The girls want to see Christmas lights so we go out cruising. One house has chimes that are playing carols. Over the top of "God Rest Ye Merry Gentlemen" Gretchen does "Away in a Manger" and gets all the words right as far as I can tell. They ought to put her on one of those telethons: it would break your heart. Then Katy does a sort of dirty version of "Jingle Bells" that I remember from when I was a kid.

Katy works the radio, spinning past the rock stations until she gets the Bucks' game.

"Hey, I didn't know you liked basketball."

"I'm on my school team."

"What position?"

"Center."

"How's the team doing?"

"They don't let us keep score, but we haven't lost yet."

"Next summer we'll find a basket and I'll show you a few moves."

"I root for the Rockets too, Dad."

"What about when they play the Bucks?"

"Well," she says, "then I hope the Bucks win one time and the Rockets win the next time."

There are a lot of fancy displays. Another house has lights all over a tree with big ornaments hanging from it and strings of little lights around what are supposed to be presents underneath. And then I remember something from my route, about this time last year. It was a medium neighborhood—a little rough around the edges but nothing bad's going to happen if your kid plays in the front yard. What it was was this house with the Christmas tree dumped off the porch with most of the decorations on it. There were presents all over the yard, every one of them still wrapped. Nobody touched the presents for the three days I delivered the neighborhood.

"I want to see my house," says Gretchen.

"Yeah, Dad."

I don't like it, but I agree as long as we don't stop.

It takes Katy a couple of false starts to get us there. The front window is outlined in lights and you can see a wreath on the door under the porch light. The rest of the house is dark and there's no car in the driveway.

"Stop," says Gretchen, "I have to go potty."

"I know where the key is," says Katy.

"No."

Back at the motel, Gretchen doesn't have to go anymore.

"I really, really did, Daddy."

"OK," I say.

"Another thing they don't have here is a swimming pool."

"Evidently," I say. "Anyway, it's December."

"But if it wasn't December you still couldn't go swimming."

"Why don't you and your sister take a little dip in the shower."

"Dad."

"Now."

Last summer Carla was driving to some teachers' convention in Denver. We worked it out so that I'd meet her in Omaha to pick up the girls. They were all in the motel pool when I got there. I hadn't seen the girls in a year. They raced over for a long, soppy cling, then jumped back in. Carla had been swimming laps; now she stood in the shallow end with Gretchen. Her hair was cut like a helmet and there was more flesh than I remembered with a tracing of blue veins on her thighs. Gretchen grabbed at her and Carla had to pull her suit back up her breasts and it really nailed me: it was like seeing a lost part of my body. It wasn't just the sex thing. We did OK that way; I've had better and I've had worse. I mean, it was my wife. She probably felt the same. Seeing her that way, I guess it was like we were married again, just for a flash.

The last night at Pizza Hut I try to make like a little celebration. The sky's the limit, I say. Katy orders her pizza with four kinds of olives and Gretchen has three Cokes. Katy points out a table in the corner. The women are laughing it up over a beer and pizza. They're wearing bowling shirts.

"Mrs. Kepplemeyer and Mrs. Smerlas teach with Mom."

Katy waves, and one of the women waggles her fingers back. A little later, the two who are facing away look around at me while pretending to look at something else. The bowling shirts say "St. Ignatius Gutter Gals." That's what she's come home to. Bingo on Wednesday night and cousins' weddings and endless squabbles about which restaurant serves the best fish fry. She wasn't like that in Oregon and she wasn't like that in Houston, but she's like that now. All the blue-collar stuff she went to college to get away from, except with a little new age mumbo jumbo tossed in. I guess teaching is pretty much blue-collar anymore. They've even got unions. She's a math teacher, and I'll bet she's good at it. Carla's got a voice like an iron gate when she needs it. I can see her drilling those smart-ass fourteen-year-olds—just bearing down on them like a gravel truck. That's what I needed when I was fourteen.

"The really, really sad part is when they shoot at him and they shoot his horse and then I just never see the horse again."

Gretchen is finishing up the plot of a TV movie.

"Tell me about Wags again."

Wags was Carla's cat who didn't come north.

"He's living with some other people now."

"Who?"

"Let's finish up here so we can open those presents."

Finally it's time for the presents. The girls told me what they wanted, so there aren't a lot of surprises. Kids don't care: they want what they want. Katy remembers to say thank you and Gretchen chips in. They both have new dolls that they're dressing up. I look for a football game on the tube but nobody's playing, so I decide to get some ginger ale at Dan's. As I'm going out the door, a woman gets out of a car two rooms down. I've seen the car off and on; maybe she lives there.

"Merry Christmas," I say.

She looks me over.

"You want something?"

"Yeah," I say. "I want you to say Merry Christmas."

"Sure," she says. And then "Merry Christmas" as she shuts the door.

Got to work on the old charm, I think. It's been a while. I suppose I should start doing that sort of thing again, but I can't seem to get around to it. After the divorce, Carla asked me if I ever slept with anyone else when we were married. Maybe she was thinking about AIDS. I almost lied, but then I didn't; I said I hadn't. She wanted to know about after Katy was born when I wouldn't do it with her. I said no, not even then. I didn't say I beat off instead. And I didn't ask her. I don't think there was anybody else, but I don't want to know.

I snuggle the girls into bed and they give me a round of kisses: butterfly kiss, fish kiss, raspberry, and finally the real thing. Katy wants me to tell a story. I'm no good at it and I've gotten around it so far but this is our last night. I still can't think of one so I start telling them about the vacation when we went camping at the Grand Canyon. Gretchen asks if she was there. She wasn't, but I know better. She comes with us in the story as a baby. The story peters out pretty soon but it's OK; they're both asleep with their dolls.

I sip some ginger ale, work my back against the old knot in it, watch the girls move in their sleep. The thing is, here I am, a grown man, and when you get right to the bottom of it I still don't understand. How can your wife love you and have your children and then change her mind? It's so simple I'm embarrassed to ask anybody.

The next morning we pack everything up except the clean clothes they'll wear to their grandma's. Then we go to Sambo's for waffles. I try to sort of wind things up, talking about next summer and how I'll call more often. I don't want to do all this at Carla's mom's. The girls aren't interested. Gretchen tries to suck up some syrup with a straw; Katy is working a puzzle on the place mat. For them, the future is after breakfast.

When we get back, there are three police cars in the motel lot and some kind of police van. The action is all down at the office, and it looks like it's over with. I park, and one of the cops comes over. I get the girls inside to change and go back to the office with him. I ask what happened and he says the manager went crazy and started blowing the place apart. He had a trip wire rigged up to a shotgun that he must have forgot about; it did a job on his legs.

"How bad?" I ask. The cop is a lot younger than me, which makes me nervous.

"I'd say his dancing days are over."

Somebody in a flak jacket sticks his head out of the living quarters.

"I haven't seen stuff like this since Nam. He's got enough ordnance in here to start WW III."

Another cop asks me a couple of questions, and I say I don't know anything. The office doesn't look in that bad a shape, but

I can see back in Wally's room where the ceiling is pretty well shot up. Then somebody yells down from the roof.

"Hey, lieutenant, there's a fucking goat up here. The guy just completely blew it away."

I ask the lieutenant if I can get back to the girls and he says sure.

The girls have been watching through the window.

"What happened, Dad?"

"The manager had an accident."

"Is he dead?"

"No."

"Will he be on television?"

"I don't think so," I say, and hustle them into their clean clothes.

The girls have forgotten about it by the time we get to Carla's mom's. She's a small woman, a little fuzzy around the edges. Bev always liked me, but I think she was ready to like whoever her daughter married. Now that we're split she has to circle the family wagons, so I don't get asked in for coffee, not that Carla would care. We stand on the porch while the girls carry things in. Bev asks about my folks, and we say what needs to be said about the weather. She's still vague, but she's on guard too; I used to tease her a lot. She can't tell that I'm all out of jokes.

The TV is already on and then it's time for hugs and kisses. I wonder if I'm going to cry, but I don't. The girls are flipping channels before I'm down the steps. I honk a couple of times before I pull out, and they both come to the window and wave.

I start crying down the block, but I'm OK by the time I catch the freeway. I've got twelve hundred miles with nothing but my past and my future to think about. What I think is this: the first time I heard hoofs on the roof of my marriage, I should have blasted away with everything I had.

Toliver

For Nat Spencer, Walter Spencer, and Mike Weltch

I first met Toliver when I'd just gotten married and had hooked up with two friends in a shirttail logging operation. He was a faller for Pope & Talbot and I'd run into him at the Dew Drop Inn after work. I had a lot of high hopes in those days; after a few beers, I could see myself turning out to be king of the woods. I had some other ideas too, but Toliver took to me anyway. He said that once life had knocked the stuffing out of me a few times, what I thought wouldn't get in my way. Besides, I tend to remind people of somebody's kid brother.

Rich and Larry and I had set ourselves up as low-tech, high-principle loggers. We had a portable sawmill, a Clark skidder (Rich drew the line at using horses to drag out the logs), a couple of fifteen-year-old trucks, and a beat-up collection of other gear. We'd all worked in the woods during college and were sure we could make a go of it doing low-impact salvage logging. I guess we saw ourselves as some kind of philosopher-loggers, bringing enlightenment to the Oregon woods.

Toliver didn't like Larry, and Rich hardly ever came in the bar, so I was the only one of us he ever had much to do with. We got on pretty well, shooting pool, talking shop—that sort of thing.

About six months after I met him, Toliver got sideswiped by the top of a buckskin hemlock snag that broke off when he dropped another tree. He was in the hospital about a month and then back and forth for the next year or so. They cobbled his leg back together, but his hip and back were pretty much shot and finally even the state workmen's comp people agreed that he was through as a faller. Toliver took a couple of gypo falling jobs but it didn't work out; word was he was slow, and a little edgy. No regular outfit would try him since he might break down on them and kick up the cost of their insurance.

Before he started drawing workmen's comp, money must

165

have been tight because his wife Janette went back to waitressing. She wanted to move to town, but Toliver said he wouldn't live where he couldn't tell who was at a bar by what rigs were in the lot.

Toliver started spending more time in the Dew Drop, since up here there's nowhere else to spend it. He greased the boredom and what must have been a lot of pain with Jack Daniels. He still used a cane sometimes, and he had to sit with his back cocked at an odd angle. Toliver was mostly ignored, which happens upriver to any man of working age who isn't working, whatever the reason. He seemed to understand this reduction the same way he knew how far any particular regular could run up his bar tab, or what kind of joke a man could make about your wife without something happening. Patterns still hold on the river; if you want to fit, you learn them and live them. I think Toliver was often drunk, but it never showed much. None of the Saturday night loudmouths ever messed with him. Even with a load of Jack Daniels, his eyes were case-hardened, and everybody knew what he had done in Vietnam.

Things went along this way while he was healing up as much as he ever would. Somewhere around then my marriage began to unravel and I started seeing more of Toliver in the evenings as well as after work. All things considered, he was pretty amiable. For a while, he even had the smile I remembered from before the accident. There's a saying upriver: "Sometimes you eat the bear; sometimes the bear eats you." Toliver's grin looked like he was always about to sit down to a meal of bearsteak.

The one thing that seemed to bother him so you could tell it was the Forest Service. Most of the land upriver, and all of the merchantable timber, belongs to the government—which in these parts means the U.S. Forest Service. Back then, I had a whole routine worked out on the Forest Service, so Toliver's resentments suited me just fine. When I got cranked up, I'd go on about how the Forest Service was just a bunch of domestic imperialists, running a colonial empire, administrators rotated

in and out to keep them from being corrupted by long associa-
tion with native customs, all the while pilfering raw materials
as though the American West was some ragtag collection of
Third World countries. I could also do a pretty fair number on
the Bureau of Land Management. You couldn't miss with the
BLM, since their management style was lifted from the Department of the Interior, which had developed its techniques
through a century of screwing the Indians out of everything.
My objections were mostly theoretical, and loggers, with their
generic distemper for rules, automatically bad-mouthed the
Forest Service. But with Toliver it was something different. All
he ever said was he never much cared for the way they did
business. I guess it was just something he didn't want to go
into, but knowing how he felt about the Forest Service helps
explain what happened later.

There was a fire crew stationed at the local ranger station,
and during fire season the crewmen spent a lot of time in the
bar. Some of the crew were college kids, looking for a little
excitement in a summer job. They'd come in wearing T-shirts
that said things like "Smokey's Friends Get High on Mountains." They were full of pranks and laughs, and you could tell
by the way they talked that they were all going to be lawyers or
businessmen or something when they grew up. This was just a
kind of grown-up summer camp for them.

Some of the crew were local boys, and they were quieter.
Their dads worked and drank and poached deer with Toliver,
so the sons knew how to behave with him. The other kids
would have been OK, but Toliver liked to crowd them—you
know, saying things like "Here comes the Forest Circus" whenever they showed up or baiting them to arm wrestle and making them say "Uncle" when he beat them. It's the only real
mean streak I ever saw in him. I wondered how he would have
acted around the Forest Service overhead, but they never
drank in the bar. Finally, the college kids stopped coming
around.

Russ, who owned the Dew Drop, wasn't real tickled that

Toliver had more or less run off some customers, but there wasn't much he could do about it. River bars have a balance to them—a kind of ecology that can only take certain kinds of change. Owners who get greedy for in-and-out business end up ruining it for everybody. They kill off the local trade, and then it's just a matter of how long their creditors will carry them before they go under. Russ had seen guys drive thirty miles to avoid going across the road to drink, so he didn't get on Toliver about the Forest Service crew.

It wasn't that Russ wouldn't get on people when they needed it. He'd been a cat skinner before he bought the bar. He had arms like yew wood from wrestling those machines all over the Cascades. Russ cut loggers the slack they needed, but if your slack ran out you weren't likely to forget it.

None of this would have amounted to anything worth mentioning if the French Pete business hadn't got mixed in, and then the whole mess set off by Harlan LeMaster. The French Pete squabble had to do with trees and jobs. The locals and the mills wanted the jobs; the city folks wanted the trees. I wanted both, so I kept my mouth shut. After about ten years of nastiness on the part of all concerned, the Forest Service had finally decided to fence off about fifty thousand acres of prime old growth timber up the French Pete drainage by adding it to the Three Sisters Wilderness Area. The Forest Service had scheduled a dedication ceremony and had invited all the factions to come bury the ax somewhere besides the back of somebody's neck. The Forest Service had managed to hack out the kind of compromise that left everybody pissed off. The environmentalists had wanted more acreage and were mad at having to sign off on two other wilderness additions to get this one. For their part, the loggers and mill owners reckoned their losses in billions of board feet. And the Forest Service was busy trying to paste their nuts back on after a decade of straddling the issue.

Still, it was Harlan LeMaster who touched off the whole concoction. Ordinarily, you wouldn't think of Harlan as primer. Harlan was mostly OK, but he hadn't been really right since a choker snapped on him. His hard hat kept him alive, but he had a plate in his head that made it tough for him to concentrate on things. He drew workmen's comp and did odd jobs: cutting up slash for firewood or cleaning creeks and digging fireline after a unit was logged.

Before the accident, Harlan would get feisty now and then when he was drunk. One time he hooked up his 4x4 to his ex-wife's trailer, hauled it down to the river, and dumped it in. The trailer floated off downstream two miles before it sank. That made an impression on everybody, especially his ex-wife, who heard about it in time to get off work at the school cafeteria and wallow along the bank beside the trailer the last quarter mile before it went down in Martins Rapids.

After the accident, Harlan was pretty quiet, but sometimes he'd get testy about some little thing. I don't know what set him off that night. He was fine when I went to the john; when I came back, Russ had 86'ed him. Nobody thought much about it, and Toliver and I went back to our shuffleboard game. But when the money ran out in the jukebox, we could hear that somebody close by was running a saw and more than that was into some serious cutting. That got everybody's attention. It was eleven o'clock at night for one thing. For another, there was no reason anybody would fire up his saw in the daylight in the Dew Drop's parking lot. So Russ stuck his head out the door, and when he came back in and got his pistol from under the bar we all piled out after him.

There was Harlan, taking down a good-sized Doug fir maybe four feet through at the butt. The fir was at the back of the lot, but it wasn't going to have any trouble reaching the bar and that's exactly where Harlan was aiming it. He'd already faced the tree and was starting on his back-cut. Besides his arms, Russ had built up his voice yelling over diesels all those years. Harlan heard him and let the saw drop back to idle.

"You get the hell away from that tree, Harlan, or I'm going to have to shoot you."

In reply, Harlan revved his McCulloch and went back to work. Russ shot twice quick, kicking up gravel near Harlan's boots, and Harlan idled the saw back down again.

"I mean it, Harlan. The next one's going into you."

By now my eyes had adjusted for the dark, but I didn't see anything that was going to help. You couldn't just run over and grab him because of the saw, and you couldn't sneak around behind because the tree was all by itself and there wouldn't have been enough time anyway. But the next thing I saw, almost like he'd come out of the ground, was Toliver about six feet in front of Harlan, standing dead in Russ's line of fire. Harlan brought the saw out of the cut and kind of waggled it at Toliver. Toliver gestured, and Harlan backed off the trigger. Like most fallers, Toliver was a little deaf, so he had a voice that carried back to us.

"Let me on around there; I'll spot you."

Harlan had kind of a screechy voice and it was harder to make him out.

"Don't need no spotter."

"Sure you do." Toliver shoved his hands into his pockets. "That top's been dead five, six years now. She's going to be coming out of there any second."

Harlan leaned back and looked up at the dark.

"Besides, you're going to need some wedges. She's fixing to swivel on you. You go to all this trouble, you might as well see it through. You ain't going to hit the bar without wedges."

Harlan thought about it, and Toliver cocked his torso in that little hitch he had to clear the pain away.

"Why you?"

"Because I'm tired of drinking in a place that throws out my friends."

"Russ is going to shoot us."

"If Russ was going to shoot anybody, he'd done it by now."

Harlan didn't say anything, so Toliver limped over the last few feet.

"Well, let's get after it."

Harlan bent back to the cut, and Toliver leaned down and popped him on the temple with his fist. Toliver's hand couldn't have moved more than a few inches and it was the side opposite where Harlan's plate was, but Harlan sat right down and then fell over.

A couple of guys hauled Harlan to his truck and stuck him inside, taking his keys. Toliver and Russ looked it over.

"She's going straight down your chimney, give or take a little."

"Goddamn him. I should've shot the little pecker. Can you turn it?"

With the saw shut down, you could hear the fir creaking in the downriver wind.

"I guess I can."

I got some wedges from my truck, and everybody else moved their rigs out of the way but around to where they could light up his work. A couple of rigs had deer lights that lit up a hundred feet or so of the trunk.

Toliver handled the Mac like it was a scalpel, paring away, revising the cut, nudging the tree with wedges. Harlan hadn't left him much wood to work with and at the end, starting its long fall, it looked all cockeyed and dead for the roof, but partway down the tree swerved on the hinge, pivoting away from the bar and coming on down like the wrath of God across the parking lot. Toliver shut the saw down and mopped his face with a bandana.

Russ told Toliver he was drinking free for the rest of the week, and somebody else said the hell with that, he was buying. An old beat-up Weyerhaeuser faller gave Toliver a hard time for taking out a section of split rail fence next to the lot.

"You got me there, Stub." Toliver grinned. "I was aiming to bring her down on your truck."

As we walked back in, Toliver stopped by Harlan's truck as though he was going to say something, but he didn't. When I left the bar at closing, Harlan was still sitting in his truck, and even though the windows were up I could hear he was crying.

That was the end of it for Harlan, but I think it was the start of it for Toliver. That fancy bit of falling must have dropped into place with his not working, the whole French Pete business, and the dedication ceremony that was coming up in about a week. All of a sudden, Toliver wasn't around. I only saw him once all week, late one afternoon at the gas station. His saw and falling gear were in the back of his truck. He looked real tired, but he moved like he wasn't hurting as much as usual. I didn't think anything about it and when I saw him again, the night before the dedication, I still didn't have any hint. The only odd thing was that he asked me to show up at the ceremony as a favor to him—made me promise, in fact—but wouldn't say why I had to be there.

So Saturday morning I drove up the East Fork. It was one of those brilliant October days when you know you are going to live forever. I went on up the Wapiti road that gave you big views of the French Pete country as you got higher up. I drove along until I got to where the Forest Service was going to put on the show. It was at a big landing above the East Fork canyon. There was an old cull deck on one edge, but the rest of the landing had been graded and they'd set up some bleachers and a sort of pavilion with tables and snacks laid out. Facing this was a little platform with chairs and a podium. They'd even brought in some portable toilets.

I hadn't been looking for anything nearly this fancy, but when everybody started showing up I could see why the Forest Service had gone to all the trouble. Senator Packwood was there, and Jim Weaver, the bristly local congressman who'd just been put on some committee that passed out money to the Forest Service. From what the newspapers said, the Forest Service big shots were peeing down their legs at the prospect of having to testify in front of him. There were twenty or so state and local politicians of various stripes and about twice that many Forest Service dignitaries including the Regional Forester and the Deputy Chief. They even had some clown stumbling around in a Smokey the Bear suit in case there were any kids. The master of ceremonies also introduced honchos from Weyerhaeuser, Georgia-Pacific, International Paper, Sierra Club, and Friends of the Earth. There were at least three television crews and lots of people taking down notes. Then there was everybody else. I'd guess there must have been two hundred of us milling around the landing by the time things got started.

To tell the truth, I was enjoying myself; you just don't see a collection like that up here. The bumper stickers were fairly predictable: "Sierra Club: Kiss My Ax" on the pickups, "Don't Californicate Oregon" on the Toyotas, "Prevent Forest Fires" and "Give a Hoot, Don't Pollute" on Uncle's gray and green fleet. The best one of all might have been "*Todo el Mundo y Yo También*" slapped across where the logo had been on what used to be a Postal Service jeep. But I couldn't tell because nobody from any of the tree planting crews was there who could have translated for me. And I'd catch snatches of conversation, things people say in a crowd as though it would all evaporate past who they were talking to.

"Next time he goes looking for money, see to it that we cut him off at the knees."

"I don't know what I'll do with the kids, but I'll think of something. Listen, I've just got to see you."

"You'd think they'd catch on. They never settle this sort of thing out of court and they keep on taking it in the shorts. It's like Mickey said: 'Never try to teach a pig to sing. It wastes your time, and it annoys the pig.'"

So I just walked around, sipping at my coffee and looking out across the canyon and on over to Sawtooth Ridge. I thought I might have picked out the clearing where I got an elk three years before. I'd just about forgotten why I'd come up in the first place when the master of ceremonies finished his introductions, which meant the speeches were close behind. Then I wondered again what Toliver had in mind. But I figured I could ride out the speeches and then go on over Wapiti and come back down the Horse Creek side so I could check out a little salvage sale we might bid on. Once I'd gone to this much trouble, Toliver would have to tell me what was going on.

I half expected them to crank up the national anthem or have some preacher invoke a blessing on the occasion. But they got right down to business. It must have been about the second speech that I realized I'd been hearing somebody running a saw for a while. In the woods, the sound of a saw is pretty much like traffic in the city; if you live there, it's something you hear but never listen to. But now I was listening because somebody had fired up a second saw and was running it full out like he was trying to limber it up. The city folks were starting to look around, and even the locals noticed because the second saw just kept running at full throttle. And it was loud. You couldn't really tell where it was coming from— mountains do funny things with sound—but it was amplified by some quirk of wind or terrain. People seemed to be glancing off across the canyon, over into the French Pete addition, and that was my guess too.

By the time the second speaker was through, the Forest Service bunch on the platform was looking real uneasy. The third speaker was Senator Packwood. He looked good: rugged, tanned, a man with power but still a man among men. I promised myself I'd give a little money to the next Democrat to run against him. The Senator had just started when a third saw fired up, again full out but at a different pitch. The Senator didn't drop a syllable as he set his notes aside.

"The sound of chain saws, the sound of men working on the weekend, remind us of why we're here today. In Oregon, we still live the American dream: that a man can work his way to the place he deserves in our society. And we know that work has no respect for calendars."

Congressman Weaver hauled out a large handkerchief and blew his nose loudly. I started edging out of the crowd so I could get a better look across the canyon. The Senator went on.

"But we also know that just as man works, he must also rest. And the magnificent landscape we come here today to honor reminds us of the recreation we earn through our labors. What finer place for thousands of men from this generation and those to come—what finer place for such men, and women, to take their leisure than the French Pete Wilderness Addition."

The first tree went down as though it had been cued. I think only the locals recognized the sound, and since it was across the canyon in a wall of firs you'd have to be looking right at a tree to see it go. Then a fourth saw pitched in, and even the Senator could tell that something was going on. People on the platform got up and started milling around. Senator Packwood left the podium to join them. The local Forest Service folks looked bad, and I saw the Deputy Chief heading for one of the portable johns. The Weyerhaeuser honcho went over, started up his truck, and began to talk to someone on his radio. The G-P man followed suit, and the Blue River District Ranger.

Five more trees went down, and now people were starting to point, trying to get their friends to see where a little space was opening up across the canyon. I hadn't picked out the spot yet, but what struck me was that all the timber going down was good-sized stuff: it was all medium-elevation old growth, and besides you could tell by the detonation every time one hit the ground. What was odd was that nobody could drop trees that big that fast. And only one saw was actually doing the cutting; the rest were just being run wide open. But the trees were going down, and I could see now that it wasn't just random; whoever was doing the falling had something in mind.

The best view was over by the platform so that's where I was. The Blue River District Ranger had come back and was talking to the Forest Supervisor. He said that the Forest helicopter was down, but that Weyerhaeuser and G-P both had ships on the way. The Forest Supervisor wanted to know the penalty for cutting timber in a wilderness area and the District Ranger told him. The Supervisor looked pleased and went over to talk to the clot of politicians. The television cameramen had driven their vans around and climbed on top to shoot. One newsman was trying to talk the lumbermen into taking his photographer up when their helicopters got there.

And the trees kept dropping: up the slope, across in a couple of rounded humps, then straight up the slope again. When the faller flattened off the top and started down, the design snapped into place. By the time he'd finished the finger, everyone recognized the universal gesture.

Somewhere along there I decided it had to be Toliver; I just couldn't figure out how. He finished the outlined hand and finger to the accompaniment of the three other saws. He'd wrapped it up and was on his way out to wherever he'd left his rig a good half hour before the first helicopter arrived. It was a slick-looking Alouette, and the Weyerhaeuser man and the District Ranger went right up. You knew they weren't going to see anything; there were millions of board feet of timber between them and Toliver, but they flew back and forth over the slope anyway. There wasn't any place to set the ship down, and it was probably too steep besides. So they came back after a while and then the Georgia-Pacific Sikorsky showed up from Oakridge. And then the ultralight, humming above the canyon like an erector set contraption somebody's weird cousin might have built.

I was on my way back to the truck when I saw the ultralight. Up the canyon it came, maybe five hundred feet above the road, an eye-watering scarlet, towing a double banner. The upper part of the banner read "Free Erma Bell." Erma Bell was one of the wilderness study areas that had been traded off to get French Pete set aside. The bottom half said "Pack Your Bags, Packwood." The ultralight circled the landing twice; then flew off upcanyon and looped around, the pilot bringing it down to maybe fifty feet off the road and heading back for us. The run was too deliberate to be just another pass, and I got over to the edge of the landing so I could bail out over the side if the guy was going to drop a bomb or something. What he dropped, though, was a load of green paint that he cut loose from a small tank by his feet. The paint floated down in a mist over the crowd, the vehicles, the pavilion and platform. It was a sort of neon green that made a nice contrast, I thought, with the gas chamber green of the Forest Service rigs.

By then the local sheriff's deputy had arrived to deal with the wilderness violation. He was bundled into the G-P Sikorsky and off they went in pursuit. The ultralight pilot decided to make a run for it, figuring that they weren't going to shoot him down for a little exterior decorating and figuring, too, that he had more air time left. As it turns out, he was right on both counts. The ultralight headed upriver, and just past Kink Creek the Sikorsky had to turn around. Since the pilot was wearing an old flight helmet and goggles, nobody ever found out who it was.

Back at the landing, people were cleaning up. The reporters were in the pavilion working on the refreshments, hanging around to see if something else was going to turn up. I saw the Deputy Chief come out of the john and walk gingerly away. The timber barons must have been relieved that the environmentalists had taken some of the heat off them with the ultralight stunt. The timber cutting would be linked to loggers, and that meant they had made Senator Packwood look bad since he was taking credit for forcing the Forest Service into the compromise. Even though the lumber industry didn't like the deal, they still expected to do business with the Senator. But the Mount Rushmore digit made them look like sore losers. Big business is all in favor of proper behavior. They'll win a lot more rounds than they'll lose, so they like to encourage good sportsmanship.

Packwood himself seemed genial enough about the whole

business, but as I was leaving I heard him talking inside the motor home he'd come up in.

"What's wrong with our local sources; why don't we have any intelligence? I can't keep track of this stuff from Washington. How the hell am I supposed to know what's going on?"

I turned around to take one more look across the canyon. The wind had freshened, and as the firs bent and returned, the finger seemed to gesture across at us.

I was in the bar that night when Toliver came in. It was Saturday night anyway, but the Dew Drop was even louder than usual because of what had happened. I'd gotten a table off in the corner and saved a chair for him. Toliver was walking gimpy, but with a kind of authority I hadn't realized he'd lost until I saw it back. It was as if he'd been turned into an imitation of himself and now he was the real thing again. He sat down and took a long pull at his beer.

"Well?"

Toliver grinned. "I think I landed a job."

"Who with?"

"I don't know yet."

"So how can you tell?"

"I did a little falling today. Tough ground, but I turned out pretty good volume. Word gets around, I expect somebody's going to figure he can use me."

Toliver wasn't going to say it right out, but I still had to know how he'd dropped so many trees so fast, so I went ahead and asked. Toliver shook some Tabasco into his beer.

"You know, Stub was telling me a while back about an old growth he came across one time. Somebody'd faced it, then stuck the wedge back in. They'd even started the back cut. Stub figured it had been that way a while by how the chips and such were all spread around. No telling how long a big tree would stand there with hardly a nip between standing and coming down."

Toliver leaned across the table and punched me on the

shoulder. He looked so tickled for a minute I thought he was going to giggle.

"You never know how it's going to come out." He was grinning like he might never stop. "Russ, bring us a couple more here and get Harlan one too."

"You ought to take a spin up the East Fork," I said. By then, I was grinning too.

"Thought I might," said Toliver. "Thought I might do just that."

A few more odds and ends turned up after the government had sifted the hillside for evidence. They found the other three saws that were running: a Husqvarna, a McCulloch, and a Stihl, all beat-up landing saws with no chains, the mufflers gone, and their triggers tied all the way down. From the cuts and the way the trees fell, they could tell it was a professional job. And that's all they ever found out officially.

Unofficially, I guess even the Forest Service finally must have heard. Pretty much everyone else on the river did. And Toliver was right about the jobs. The cutting boss at Pope & Talbot told him he'd take him back in a minute but the overhead would have his hide if they ever found out. It was the medium-sized outfits that were ornery enough to hire him, hang productivity or insurance or political consequences. Toliver got three offers, but he finally went with Santini Brothers because Frank and Joey themselves came in one night to ask him.

I don't get up the East Fork much anymore. Lately, though, I've been going out just driving, and last week I ended up over that way. It was late April with the snow still patchy in the shade and the road not open over Wapiti yet. I turned out at the landing and looked across. After sifting the regulations, the Forest Service had decided that they couldn't cut any trees to edit the offending scene. What they'd done instead was to plant some special Doug fir seedlings, genetically engineered for quick growth. In the muted spring light, the new needles on the seedlings lit up the hillside. The great finger rose above them, the mature blue-gray of the old growth outlined in electric green.

I hadn't seen much of Toliver for a while. I'd stopped drinking to see if Amy and I could keep it going, so I didn't hang out at the Dew Drop. After Amy left, I went down one night for a rip-roarer and made an ass of myself. It was Toliver who hauled me home.

"You never know how it's going to come out, right?"

He'd got me in the house and was on his way out.

"That's right," he said. He turned around at the door and looked me over. "But sometimes it don't hurt to take a hint."

I thought about that, parked there on the landing. I'd meant to ask Toliver what the hint was, but the time for asking had passed. Amy was gone, Rich was gone, and Larry and I were tearing the sheets. I kept looking across, trying to leave another piece of the country so it would all be gone before I pulled out. Against the grain of memory, Toliver rose up then, the grin pouring across his face. And I stockpiled that spreading smile—the hell with traveling light. I thought if I turned it right, I could sight down it to calculate my line of fall.

Other Iowa Short Fiction Award and John Simmons Short Fiction Award Winners

1988
The Long White,
Sharon Dilworth
Judge: Robert Stone

1988
The Venus Tree,
Michael Pritchett
Judge: Robert Stone

1987
Fruit of the Month, Abby Frucht
Judge: Alison Lurie

1987
Star Game, Lucia Nevai
Judge: Alison Lurie

1986
Eminent Domain, Dan O'Brien
Judge: Iowa Writers' Workshop

1986
Resurrectionists, Russell Working
Judge: Tobias Wolff

1985
Dancing in the Movies,
Robert Boswell
Judge: Tim O'Brien

1984
Old Wives' Tales,
Susan M. Dodd
Judge: Frederick Busch

1983
Heart Failure, Ivy Goodman
Judge: Alice Adams

1982
Shiny Objects, Dianne Benedict
Judge: Raymond Carver

1981
The Phototropic Woman,
Annabel Thomas
Judge: Doris Grumbach

1980
Impossible Appetites,
James Fetler
Judge: Francine du Plessix Gray

1979
Fly Away Home, Mary Hedin
Judge: John Gardner

1978
A Nest of Hooks, Lon Otto
Judge: Stanley Elkin

1977
The Women in the Mirror,
Pat Carr
Judge: Leonard Michaels

1976
The Black Velvet Girl,
C. E. Poverman
Judge: Donald Barthelme

1975
*Harry Belten and the
Mendelssohn Violin Concerto,*
Barry Targan
Judge: George P. Garrett

1974
*After the First Death There Is
No Other,* Natalie L. M. Petesch
Judge: William H. Gass

1973
The Itinerary of Beggars,
H. E. Francis
Judge: John Hawkes

1972
The Burning and Other Stories,
Jack Cady
Judge: Joyce Carol Oates

1971
Old Morals, Small Continents,
Darker Times,
Philip F. O'Connor
Judge: George P. Elliott

1970
The Beach Umbrella,
Cyrus Colter
Judges: Vance Bourjaily
and Kurt Vonnegut, Jr.